Star's Odyssey.

© Clint Green 2024

1. Prologue

Alex awoke to the dreaded sound of hissing and clicking that had become hauntingly familiar to him. It was starting again. The chill that covered his body hit at first as his senses woke one by one. His skin prickled, and he sensed the dull ache where his left leg used to be. The coldness of the glass against the stump at the end of his right arm. The pressure of the restraints, biting into his skin.

The smell came next, that acrid scent of steel and rotting leaves, that was the only thing he could relate it to. It seeped into his nostrils; the fear creeping into him with it. A sudden rush of adrenaline sharpened his focus. He knew what he would see next and willed himself to close his eyes, but his body disobeyed. No matter how hard he tried, he wouldn't be able to move this time, no more than he could the previous times.

As his vision cleared, the room slowly came into view. He was there again, the other man. Hanging in his suspension tube opposite Alex. The man had sandy blond hair that was shaved, and Alex could see a section on the side of his head where his skull was partially exposed. One of his eye sockets was empty and a small trail of blue liquid seeped out like an iridescent tear. His other eye stared wildly and locked onto Alex's own.

They had only spoken once before, and the others took that ability away from them quickly after that. No names. Nothing more than a rushed string of words from the other man.

"Hey, Hey, buddy it's ok. It's ok. Focus on me. Look me in the eye and don't look around. HEY BUDDY! You. Look at me. It's gonna to be ok. Just focus on me and don't show any pain. Don't let them…." and then it was gone.

That was the first time he had seen the creatures, their captors. The first time he lost his mind in fear, confusion, and helplessness. The second time was no better. Alex couldn't count the times they had woken him up from whatever stasis they held him in, and each time, he and the man wordlessly faced each other and tried to bear what was to come.

The man's eye flickered sideways briefly, then bored into Alex's own. Alex felt this heart beat faster as he knew that the man has seen the creature coming and if the man had seen it, then it was coming for Alex. A shadow fell across his face and the fine hair covering his arm and the sensitive stump of freshly healed skin rose. He felt a coldness touch his side, and he wondered what they would take this time. Forcing his eyes open, he looked at the creature's face, emotionless beneath a breathing mask and goggles. He took in the familiar grey, scarred skin and then…Darkness.

Alex awoke again for the twentieth time. As the blur cleared from his eyes, he looked over to the Sandy haired man and his breath caught in his throat. The man was there, suspended in his tube, arms pinned to the wall, but at the base of his torso there was nothing. His legs had been removed completely and the end of his spine trailed below. There was no blood, no viscera. Everything was smooth and sealed except for the bone of his spine dangling below, just beneath the ribcage.

Even worse, something had completely removed the man's brain, cut open his skull, and replaced it with wires and more of the metallic blue liquid. The man stared lifelessly ahead, almost in a mockery of the eye contact they used to make. Alex started with a shock as he realised they had meticulously healed his eye at some point and replaced it in his socket. He couldn't fathom why they would do that if they were just going to kill him anyway.

He felt the sheer sense of loss and desperation shudder through him and the tightness along his side meant that they had taken something from him too, but too paralysed by the machine to move or feel pain. He could only guess at what. As he breathed deeper, trying to calm himself any way he could, Alex slowly became aware that the room was deathly quiet. None of the clicks of hissing that usually accompanied an awakening, none of the movement he could usually sense off to the sided and no smell of mulch and metal. What was different?

As his breathing slowed and he resolutely avoided looking at the man opposite him, he realised he was the only one here, the only one awake. He didn't know how many more people were trapped here with him, but he could only see the now dead man and the sight of the edge of another suspension tube next to him, hinting at there being many more victims.

His heart beat now almost back to normal. Alex concentrated on listening to the room around him for any sign of someone entering, but still nothing. His mind raced as to what could have happened, but then there was a click and a bubbling sound as he felt the anaesthetic once again work its way into his system.

As sleep gently took him again, Alex wondered briefly if the creatures were not there, who had woken him?

Alex awoke again, startled and fresh. He felt different this time. He had woken much easier than before and felt more alert. Bracing himself to see the body of his only friend here, his eyes widened when he saw that the man was gone. In his place was someone new, some-thing new. She was humanoid, maybe a little shorter than the average human woman, but fine golden fur covered her entire body.

Her lips were humanlike, but thin, and her nose flatter and tapered up to her dark almond-shaped eyes which flickered with fear as she awoke for maybe the first time. Swept up from above her eyes were goat like horns ribbed and curved back to a wicked point but marred by similar restraints to the ones on his arms to hold her steady. She thrashed against the restraints uselessly and panted in horror as she realised her situation.

The alien woman looked at him as she realised he was awake and her eyes widened more. Alex couldn't be sure if she feared him or what they had done to him. He desperately wished he could give her the same speech he had received, some solace in this dark place, but even if he could physically speak, he was too emotionally numb to inspire anyone and he knew it was unlikely they could understand each other.

He watched the woman tense as suddenly the creature came into view. One metallic hand reached up to touch the woman's horn and the other hand, grey and scarred, lifted a machine up towards her face. It hit a switch, and the machine buzzed into life, a whirring metal blade spinning faster and faster. Alex had never seen one in action before and he inadvertently let out a gasp of horror as he realised what was about to happen.

At the sound of Alex's inhale, the creature spun around and its eyes widened beneath the goggles, obviously surprised to see Alex awake. It shambled towards him and thumped the panel on Alex's machine until the click and bubble of the Anaesthesia slowly took him away into the dark again.

2. Awakening

The smell of smoke, acrid and hot, hit Alex as he snapped awake. The room was darker than usual and a haze hung in the air. Alex realised that his suspension tube was open and the sound of an alarm weakly blazing beat through the space. He wiped his eyes to clear the tears that had welled up from the irritation of the smoke and stopped. Then it hit him. He wasn't restrained and had wiped his eyes with the hand they had removed. He stared down at his hand, it's too white skin standing out from the rest of his arm, but no scarring at his wrist whatsoever.

He shifted, the discomfort from not having moved for so long fighting against the very fact that he COULD. He stepped forward weakly, without thinking, and his bare foot hit the cold wet floor. His leg was back too, the same pale white as his hand, but still muscular and firm. Amazed, Alex was staring at his feet when a prickle at the back of his neck reminded him where he was and he looked around the room, startled.

Chaos met his gaze as he saw the room for the first time. It was smaller than he had imagined, containing around 8 tubes like his, 3 of which were toppled over onto the floor, mangled and crushed by a large beam of metal and white that had fallen from the ceiling.

"Hello 574." A female voice rang out clearly above the failing alarm, making Alex start."Please do not be afraid. I am not the ones that took you"

"Who?" Alex gasped out, his voice raw from disuse and smoke inhalation. "Who are you? What is 574?"

"I'm sorry, I only know you by their designation. Asset 574. Do you have a name?" The voice was crisp and gentle, like a nurse. No nonsense, but reassuring at the same time.

"Um, I'm Alex. I can't see you. Where are you? Do you have a name too?" He stared around the room, trying to locate the voice, but it seemed to come from everywhere. Apart from the ones smashed on the floor, the other tubes remained sealed, but the condition of them and the quantity of what he assumed was blood and other fluids seeping from them suggested it was unlikely anything was still alive underneath.

"I am," The voice paused briefly "In another location, speaking to you via the inter-ship communication devices," another pause "I am afraid my name doesn't translate well into your language, the nearest approximation would be 'They who seeks the stars and leaves home behind without pause,' but you can call me Star if you like."

"Star. It's nice to hear another voice. So, when you say my language, I take it you are not human?"

"Human, is that the name of your species?"

"Yeah, that's what we call ourselves."

"Then no, I am not human. Neither were those that took you, or those in the surrounding tubes currently. There is one other human already with me, who is eager to meet you, but I would appreciate you freeing Assets 260 and 762 before you join us as their tubes have been badly damaged and their vital signs are fluctuating. I am quite concerned about their wellbeing."

Alex looked at the tube next to him, where the horned woman was. He could see she was awake and panicking, but still shackled to the wall.

"How do I open these? What do I do?" Alex choked out as he tried to make sense of the control panel in front of the tube.

"I need you to press the central button on the middle row and then quickly press the circular icon on the screen. That should remove 762's shackles and open the tube. Then open the tube behind you and to your left, the male inside, that is 260."

Alex hurriedly pressed the button and screen as asked and as soon as the tube slid open, he turned and did the same on the other tube. The occupant was male, with a silver sheen to his skin and deep blue hair and brows. He too, was awake and staring at Alex calmly as if this was just another day.

"Star, how will they understand me? I don't want to scare them."

"I can understand you perfectly." The silver man whispered. "Thank you for freeing me."

"Please! Please! What is happening? Where are we?" came a feminine voice from behind him.

Alex startled at the two aliens speaking in clear English. The man sounded like an aristocrat, and the woman spoke with what sounded like a Northern English accent.

Star's voice rang out from above "Apologies. When I had you repaired, I took the liberty of making some changes, including implanting a universal translation device into each of you as well as a mild anti-anxiety solution to help with any psychological issues in the short term."

The woman went still and reached up to touch her head. An expression of disgust across her face, but the Silver man seemed to take it in his stride.

"Interesting procedure. I usually have to pay for any work I get done! Maybe once we get out of this hellhole, I can talk to you about further work? I have a list, you see…"

"Is that why I'm not freaking out?" Alex interrupted. "Because I feel like I should be freaking out. Hell, I feel like I should be freaking out about not freaking out."

"Yes." Star said, "Your fear response will be temporarily number, but wit will not affect your reaction time or cognitive ability."

"Great. Freakout postponed until later. We should still get out of here before those creatures come back. Star, can you guide us to you?"

"I can indeed, Alex, and do not worry about those 'creatures', as you say. They have been taken care of. I am going to create a trail for you to follow to reach me. Just follow the lights and you will be fine."

The Silver man startled at this. "They took care of the Vrexen? That is quite a feat. Whoever our esteemed rescuer is, they must be eminently capable,"

"What are the Vrexen?" The woman spoke softly, curiously and with a hint of panic still underlying her tones despite the drugs. "What are YOU? Where are we and what is happening?"

"My name is J'Coub," said the silver man as he looked at the woman for the first time. "I am from the Aynaud System. My species, well, we are known as Courions."

Alex looked at the man and nodded a greeting. "I'm Alex. Human and from a planet called Earth,"

The woman stepped back slightly and steeled herself against the wall. "I don't understand? I have never heard of these places? I have never seen anyone like you at all. Where in the world are you from? Beyond the seas??"

"Oh, dear" Said J'Coub. Then whispered in an exaggerated aside to Alex, "What do you think? Primitive Race? Non space-faring?"

Alex looked at him and spread his hands. "Don't ask me. My people haven't even left the solar system yet. But at least most of us believe in life on other planets." He stared at the two unfamiliar creatures, an itch at the back of his brain telling him how insane this scenario was.

"I'm sorry. It's just, I never thought I would ever meet actual aliens. I must look strange to you as well." He said.

"You look like someone took every bipedal species in the galaxy, merged them all together, then took all the interesting bits out." J'Coub sniffed. The woman only whimpered.

Alex went to respond and thought better of it. He turned to the woman. "I'm so sorry. This must be even more confusing to you than it is to me, but let's get somewhere safe before we talk about this sci-fi shit any further." He held out a palm calmingly and looked around for the lights that Star mentioned.

He saw an uneven line of yellow glowing lights along the floor and pointed to the others. "I guess we follow the Yellow Brick Road!"

J'Coub snorted in frustration. "Great, TWO primitives. Those are lights. That's a corridor, and that is a metal floor, not brick." He said with exaggerated slowness. "Oh and the Vrexen, since the lovely lady asked, are almost a myth. A cautionary tale for space travellers and planet dwellers alike."

"A myth?" Alex asked.

"Yes, as in 'Don't go out alone or the Vrexen will get you'. There have only been two verified encounters with them, as far as I know. Scavengers, kidnappers, murderers and brutes. No two ships alike as far as we can tell and all a mixture of technology and organics. It's quite interesting, in fact…"

Alex gently guided the two towards the lights. "What are you? A scientist?" He said as the trio began cautiously moving into the corridor.

J'Coub laughed bitterly. "No. Despite my family wishing I were, I actually run an art gallery and cafe. But growing up with scientist in our unit, you learn a thing or two despite being a massive disappointment to them."

Alex nodded, heartened by the strange familiarity with the alien's story. "I'm a Carpenter. Someone who, er, makes things out of wood. I was coming back from a job when they took me. All I saw was a bright light surrounding me and then nothing until I woke up the first time in that damn tube"

"A woodman! I know woodmen from my tribe. They make beautiful things," said the woman, obviously happy to find a sense of familiarity in this strange situation. "My name is Sorah. I tend the herds. The light appeared to me too, and I ran towards it to keep it away from the young."

Alex smiled in response, happy that Sorah was attempting to fit in with them."Well, it's nice to meet you Sorah. That sounds like a brave thing you did and I am sure that the, er, young are fine."

"It is my duty, not bravery, that made me act Alex of the Human Tribe. It is my sacred honour to protect our children at any cost and to kill all that threaten them. Also, the bugs are now moving to our left." She pointed out casually.

"Light's not bugs, my dear. I see your education will be a challenge, but I assure you I am up to the task!" J'Coub waved his hand around airily.

Alex inspected the path they were embarking on. "No, I think it is your turn to learn, J'Coub. They really are insects! They almost look like fireflies from my planet."

J'Coub sniffed in distaste. "You are quite right. Or Sun Beetles from my home world. How strange. Well, never say I am one who will not admit when he is wrong! Let's follow the disgusting things, whatever they are."

The corridor they entered was not what Alex had expected when he imagined an alien ship. None of the bright clean lines from familiar sci-fi shows and films. Rough, pale walls dotted with imperfections stretched ahead. Occasionally, computer panels or large metal struts interrupted the flow. Bizarre pulsating pipes, resembling large veins, were between the top of the walls and the ceiling. Alex ran his hand down the wall, surprised to find it pliant and warm.

The Trio continued in silence as they passed through the ship. The dire situation they were in forcing a camaraderie made of necessity, an attempt to find something familiar and safe in the madness that surrounded them. They had not progressed far before they came upon the first body.

Alex and J'Coub stopped in their tracks at the sight of one of the Vrexen strewn across the hallway, it's still form reaching towards the doorway as if it had died in a vain attempt to escape. Sorah strode forward and without pause stomped on the creature's head, driving a hoof through its skull with a powerful ease. Alex and J'Coub stepped back in alarm, but Sorah just shrugged weakly and said, "It is best practice to make sure that the viper is dead before it has time to strike again."

"I'm just glad to see you are less afraid, Sorah." said Alex reassuringly.

Sorah smiled sadly at that. "I am always afraid Alex of Human Tribe. My people are prey. There are so many things that threaten us, we are driven by fear. To flee, to run from everything! But even though my body trembles with the urge to escape and my hands shake constantly and my heart beats in my throat, I try to turn that fear into action I can use. They chose me to protect our young for that reason. Because even though my body screams at me to flee, I choose to fight." She looked down at the body beneath her and shuddered. "Even now, when I do not know half these things you say and this building looks like none I have seen before, I will be afraid and I will embrace that fear and use it to survive."

J'Coub and Alex stared at Sorah for a beat before Alex replied, "Then let's all embrace that fear and help each other survive." He nodded to them both, and they left the ruined body behind and continued through the ship.

Whatever had happened had left huge portions of the ship in ruins and the trail of small light creatures shifted and changed as it took them on roundabout routes through the chaos. Other areas of the vessel seemed untouched to Alex's eye, but the confusing layout and Frankenstein like design were hard to understand.

"This place is insane." J'Coub said as he stepped over yet another body. A look of distaste on his handsome face. "It doesn't look like any other ship I have ever been on."

"This whole situation is insane." Sorah responded. "I would say I was having a nightmare, but this is beyond anything I could ever imagine."

Alex stopped in his tracks. "Er, guys? Is it just me, or is that wall over there breathing?"

3. Bare Bones

"You are nearing your destination, the Bridge." Star's voice rang out through the corridor as the trio emerged into a wider room with a door just ahead of them. Ignoring Alex's statement, they all looked ahead. The large, heavy door stood slightly ajar, sparks emerging erratically from one side. Moving cautiously through the door, a scene of controlled chaos greeted the team.

The walls of the room curved organically, reminiscent of the ribcage of a giant creature, with a texture that looks like bone or hardened coral, integrated with panels of smooth, dark metal and glowing screens, some of which are now flickering erratically. The high ceiling arched overhead in a spine-like formation, with bioluminescent nodules providing a soft, ambient light, now dimming in places. Along the front of the space, shutters covered an entire wall, blocking off the viewscreen from whatever danger the ship had encountered.

In the centre of the room, a large holographic table flickers between images of star maps and static. Cracks mar the surface of the table, while an automated extinguishing system is busy putting out a small, contained electrical fire, leaving behind the smell of burnt wiring.

To one side, there's a bank of control panels, some hanging off their hinges, with exposed wires sparking. A few panels are still operational, showing vital statistics of the ship, including damage reports, and a human woman stood there cursing as she kicked the wall.

"Shanice, I don't believe we can repair those systems by kicking them into working order." Star's voice rang out, clearer now from the other side of the room. Alex gaped at what appeared to be a living wall, part of the ship's organic system. The same flesh as the corridor, clearly damaged and displaying what appeared to be gills, slowly released an amber Sap-like fluid from wounds and scratches. As Star's voice spoke, lights within the wall pulsed in time with each word.

The woman sighed in frustration and turned around to face the newcomers. Her dark skin marred by soot and fluids, but her eyes shone as her anger softened into something akin to relief. "Oh, my god! It's such a relief to see you all awake!" she said. "Its just been me and Star for the last week since the attack and as sweet as she is, I still feel like I am going a little crazy talking to the walls!"

J'Coub startled at that. "A week? What attack?"

Shanice grimaced and gestured to some benches around the central table. They looked to be functional rather than comfortable and appeared moulded into the floor itself. "Please, take a seat. I think Star and I have some explaining to do."

As the group slowly took a seat, Sorah held back slightly before joining them. She looked around the bridge with a mix of wonder and fear. She perched lightly on the edge of one bench, looking for all the world like she would bolt at any moment.

"You're human too?" Alex asked as he took a seat. Surprisingly, the hard-looking bench gave way slightly beneath him and moulded perfectly to his rear, making a cushioned base. "Oh, this is weirdly comfortable!"

Shanice smiled in response. "Sure am. Peckham born and bred! Star tells me they took us at the same time, but for some reason, they kept me on a different part of the ship. They, um, hadn't done anything to me yet, so Star woke me up first, as I didn't need any healing. It's been a wild ride."

"I see. Well, whatever you did to heal us, Star, I must say I am immensely grateful to have my penis back. Oh, and my feet, I suppose," J'Coub interjected gleefully. "Those wrinkled grey scrotes took something new every time they woke me up." He shuddered in recollection.

"Are we the only ones left?" Alex asked. "I saw other pods in the main room, some damaged, but others past the wreckage looked complete?"

Shanice placed her hands on the table and the holographic image flickered slightly and then went off. "We are the only ones left alive. Sort of." She paused briefly. "There is one other to bring round, but it's more complicated than we were." She leant back in the seat and took a breath. "The whole situation is weirder than you think. Let me explain..."

"The Vrexen were more than scavengers. They took ships, technology, and biological specimens. Assets, they called us. They stripped everything for parts and incorporated it into this ship and their technology, including us."

"If a piece of technology did something clever, they wired it into the ship," she continued, her voice tinged with a mix of awe and sorrow. "And it wasn't just technology; they did the same with living beings. Star IS the ship. She was once a living being herself. Forgive me Star, but imagine a mix between a giant space squid and a whale, I guess from the images she showed me."

"They integrated bones, muscles, and sensory organs from different creatures into Star herself. Anything they could re-use or re-purpose. Star, do you want to tell your story?" She asked suddenly, "I don't want to get anything wrong here."

The wall that Alex had initially thought Star 'lived' in pulsed gently with light. "Thank you Shanice, I would be happy to share my tale, but I am afraid time is against us, so please forgive me for being brief. Hopefully, we will all have time to share tales soon." The wall glittered up and down with soft amber lights before Star spoke again.

"Shanice," Star's voice, a soft and neutral tone, emanated from the ship's communication system. "Shanice," its words carefully chosen, "I have observed that this environment can be quite... formidable for those unaccustomed to the vastness of space. Sorah, being new to these experiences, might find a more serene setting conducive to understanding her new reality. Perhaps the observation lounge? Its views are expansive yet comforting, and the setting might ease her into the concepts of space travel and our current predicament."

Shanice smiled and nodded. "Yeah, I think a talking spaceship might be a bit much straight away." She stood and offered Sorah her hand. "Come with me Sorah, let's get some food and I can explain what is going on." Sorah stood and warily took Shanice's hand, meekly following her off the Bridge.

Star's compassion and understanding struck Alex unexpectedly. "Thank you Star, that was well done."

J'Coub nodded in acknowledgement. "Indeed, now that it's just us boys and, um, Star! Shall we continue? Only. the mention of food made me rather hungry."

Star's systems made what sounded like a chuckle. "It would be my pleasure. As Shanice said, my species evolved to move through the vacuum of space. We travel instinctively from star to star where we meet in the sun's warmth to share song-stories, mate and raise our young." Star paused briefly as if taking a breath and the wall swelled gently. "We encountered other species occasionally but were happy to live our lives as they were, mostly keeping to ourselves. My kind can weave gateways in space to move from system to system, other species highly coveted this, and they killed many of our kind in ages past to replicate this skill technologically until it proved impossible for them and they learned to leap between the stars in other ways."

"I'm so sorry Star, that sounds horrific!" J'Coub stared at the wall in sympathy.

"Thank you J'Coub," Star replied. "It was many generations ago and since then, my kind has been left mostly in peace. We have changed our ways to be warier of others and never stray near inhabited systems."

"I was young when the Vrexen took me and was completely naïve to the dangers that could lurk in the dark of space. I had wandered alone, away from my pod. Dreaming in the void of many things, pulsars and nebulas and the wonders I had seen." Star sighed. "and then I felt an impact on my back. I thought at first I had lazily floated into the path of a comet, the pain was so severe, but then I felt movement and more pain as they bored into my skin and begun working through my flesh, cutting and hacking and implanting things within me."

"It was a torment unlike any I had experienced," Star continued, her voice resonating with a mixture of pain and resilience. "They were relentless, these Vrexen. Seeing in me not a living being but a vessel to be exploited, a means to traverse the stars. They carved me up, integrating their technology into my body, forcing me to become something I was not. It violated my very essence, a fusion of their mechanical monstrosities with my young body."

Alex listened, his heart heavy with empathy. "They turned you into a ship," he whispered, the horror of Star's experience sinking in.

"Yes, Alex," Star responded. The walls of the ship seemed to pulse with a sadness that was almost tangible. "They reshaped me, bound me to their will, and used my natural abilities for their own ends. I became a living prison, not just for myself but for others like you, captured and tormented for the Vrexen's purposes."

"But how did you gain control? How did you break free from them?" J'Coub asked, his voice tinged with both curiosity and concern.

"It was a slow process," Star explained. "Over time, I learned to interface with the technology they implanted in me and also the biologics. Bit by bit, I reclaimed control of my body. It was not just a physical struggle, but a mental one. To assert my will over the invasive systems took centuries, but eventually, I mostly succeeded, except for the control device they used to force my obedience. They implanted computer systems made from hundreds of brains of many species, all interwoven. I learned to speak to them in a fashion and we kept each other sane."

"And then last week, an unknown enemy attacked us. In only seconds, I felt hundreds of missiles strike me, doing untold damage. Even the metal scales they had wrapped me in could not prevent the devastation. Amidst the pain and the shock, though, I felt a strange sense of peace. I thought I was dying and briefly welcomed the thought of death. But this peace came not from the embrace of the void. One missile had hit and destroyed the control unit used to enslave me."

"As my systems failed one by one, I used what time I had to weave a gate somewhere far away and as soon I was safely on the other side... Well, I turned against the Vrexen, determined to free myself and any others they had trapped. So I released a toxin throughout my interior, deadly only to the Vrexen, and I killed them all."

The two of them reacted to Star's revelation with a mix of awe and sombre understanding. The thing they were currently sitting in was not just a ship, but a being with a tragic past, a survivor of unspeakable atrocities and a fellow victim of the Vrexen's cruelty.

Star spoke again after a quiet pause. "Then I woke Shanice, set her to fixing you all up and now we are here."

Silence filled the room. Neither Alex nor J'Coub knew what to say. Alex's life had been completely turned upside down, and despite trying to project calmness aided by whatever drug Star had given him, inside his mind was reeling.

Inside the tube where he had been held captive, he had come to understand what had happened to him, sort of resigned himself to the reality of it. But held there, he had no choice. Now he was free and not just focused on surviving the next few minutes, the weight of it all pressed down on him hard.

"Star, I…" Alex took a moment to steady himself. "I'm so sorry to hear what you went through. This whole situation is…horrific…What we have all been through? It's too much."

It was J'Coub, who reached across the table and placed a steady hand on Alex's arm. "Alex. I know. Believe me, I know. But I also know we are in a better position now than we were so recently. All we can do is focus on the here and now and the short-term future." He gripped Alex's wrist where the pale flesh of his new hand met the fading tan of his arm. "On my planet, we have a saying. 'If the Baratosh is too big to eat in one bite, simply break it into smaller mouthfuls." He grinned and nodded his head wisely.

Alex felt his firm hand grip his wrist and then release. The alien then patted his hand like a parent would a child. "What's a Baratosh? Why is this relevant?" He asked.

"oh, um. A Baratosh is a large fruit. It grows to immense sizes and is a traditional meal on my planet. It's not that nice, really. I can't stand the stuff unless it's fermented into wine, of course. But you are missing the point. What it means is, if something is too large and overwhelming, you break it down into smaller pieces and just focus on what you can do. Bit by bit you do each one and then you have eaten the whole damn fruit. Or solved the problem."

J'Coub waved his hands in the air in what Alex could only interpret as some kind of bizarre alien jazz hands. It was that bizarre yet familiar gesture that really broke through to Alex as much as the good advice that he recognised from some of the therapy sessions he had been through on Earth. He nodded and smiled. "Thanks J'Coub. You're right. They said something similar to me when I left the Army. Coming back to civilian life after war can be overwhelming too."

J'Coub started at that, and his grey eyes narrowed slightly. "A Warrior? I thought you said you worked wood?"

Alex laughed gently. "Oh, I do. I was injured in a battle and couldn't return to service. I wasn't even in service that long. 24 years old and already medically retired."

"That is terrible! I can't imagine what it would be like. A brave young soldier taken down in his prime by enemy fire, heroically placing himself in danger for others." J'Coub clutched his chest, and Alex laughed as he practically swooned.

"I wish it was that dramatic or even heroic!" said Alex, shaking his head slightly. "Truth is, I fell off a bloody roof." He snorted lightly. "Walked backwards to get away from the enemy line of sight, tripped on my bleeding pack and hit the floor. Rolled straight off the roof and knackered my back in!"

J'Coub's eyes softened, then crinkled with amusement and sympathy. "You..you tripped and rolled off a roof in the middle of a battlefield?" He broke into a grin. "What kind of warrior were you?"

Alex smiled back at him. "A young one! Just an infantryman in way over his head, really. Anyway, got myself invalided out of the Army. Took a while to recover and then I had to adjust to civvy life. Started doing bits of carpentry here and there to keep my hands and mind busy, just small stuff."

Star's voice chimed in. "I think you will find that I have repaired the damage to your spine, hip, shoulder and ankle when I was healing you from your other injuries. I also took care of your deteriorating eyesight, mild hearing loss, and various smaller issues."

Alex's eyes widened as he started to take note of his body and the previously unobserved lack of that familiar ache he had grown used to. He reached down to his side, and the once scarred skin now felt smooth and warm under his touch. "Star, you are bloody amazing! How can I ever thank you for that? How can I ever repay you? You don't know what this means to me!"

There was a beat before Star spoke. "I know what it is like to lose parts of yourself, Alex. I understand all too well. There is too little of me left to regain what I once was. The least I can do is help you all." Her voice had a wistful tone to it. "As for repayment, all I ask is you all help me repair as much damage from the attack as possible so we can work out our next steps. Currently, my systems are deteriorating at a rapid rate. Without your aid, we will all be stranded here until we slowly die."

4. Tick..Tick...Tick

"What in the name of the 19 Sisters is THAT?" J'Coub exclaimed loudly.

Alex stared at the table before them. "It looks dangerous."

Shanice sighed and gestured towards the table. "It's fine! Stop being such babies and trust me on this one."

"I don't believe it is harmful." Came Sorah's voice from the other side of the observation room, where she sat hugging her knees and staring out into the vastness of space with a look of wonder on her face.

Shanice sighed. "Guys, it's FOOD. I have been eating it all week and I promise you it goes in and comes back out just like it should. I feel fine. It's a nutrient meal that the Vrexen ate." She gestured again at the two bowls on the table in front of them.

Alex and J'Coub had joined Sorah and Shanice in the Observation room, now doubling up for the team as makeshift rec-room and dining area. Untouched by the ravages of the battle, it beautifully melded the ship's unique organic and technological characteristics. The room was spacious, with high, curved ceilings that follow the natural, flowing design of Star's body.

Sorah was examining a wall, formed of a transparent membrane that offered a breathtaking, panoramic view of the star-studded expanse of space outside.

The furniture in the room looked minimalistic yet comfortable, with seating arrangements that include cushioned chairs and benches arranged in a semi-circular fashion facing the large window with a low table between them all.

Soft and ambient lighting, coming from bioluminescent panels in the ceiling lit the space, casting a calming glow over various plants that looked like they could be part of Star's organic systems. They added a touch of greenery and vitality that Sorah also seemed fascinated by.

Alex tentatively brought a spoonful of the bright green mush to his nose and sniffed carefully before turning to J'Coub. "Well mate, I will if you will"

J'Coub started in surprise. "Alex. You seem very nice, but I don't recall mating with you! Did something happen in the tubes that I don't remember? OH Skies! Was it before or after they took my penis? Was I any good?"

Alex made a puzzled face before Shanice broke in with laughter. "J'Coub, um, on our world. Well, in our part of the world we come from, England. Mate is a slang term for a friend."

"Oh!" J'Coub exclaimed. "How strange you humans are. Why not just say friend then? In that case, Alex, I would happily call you a friend as well. But I am not ruling out mating with you either, it just seems a terribly inappropriate time!"

Alex's eyed widened, and he stammered out. "Well, um, I suppose I am flattered? Thanks J'Coub. But I meant the food. Shall we give it a go?"

"I assure you it is completely edible and poses no threat to any of your individual biological systems." Star said from the ceiling above. "Also, as you may have noticed, the Universal Translation System adapts as it goes along, so there may be occasional errors in translation between your various languages."

Star's voice carried a tone of both pride and solemnity. "The universal translator integrated into each of you is a marvel of biological and technological synthesis. It's composed of neural tissues and sensory organs from a variety of species, each selected for their exceptional linguistic and pattern recognition abilities."

Alex looked intrigued. "So, it's like a biological computer?"

"In a way, yes," Star continued. "For example," Star continued, "the neural tissues of the Zarnak from Cygnus-5 possess extraordinary auditory pattern recognition, enabling them to comprehend and imitate intricate sounds and languages."

"And the visual component?" Shanice asked, clearly fascinated.

"The visual processing relies on the ocular cells of the Vortaxians from Andromeda-3, a species with a remarkable ability to interpret visual symbols and written languages, even those they've never encountered before. Their cells can detect subtle patterns and extrapolate meaning from them."

"What about the actual translation process?" J'Coub inquired.

"That's where artificial intelligence comes in," Star explained. "The biological components provide raw data processing, but the AI integrates these inputs, comparing them against a vast database of known languages. It's constantly learning, adapting to new linguistic nuances it encounters."

Sorah looked thoughtful. "So, you say that this is a tribe, almost? A mix of many minds meeting?"

"Exactly," Star affirmed. "It's a testament to the diversity of life in the universe and our ability to create harmony from disparate elements. The translator doesn't just convert words; it interprets context, cultural nuances, and even emotions to some extent, bridging the gap between species."

"Fascinating!" J'Coub pondered over the almost revolutionary process that this must have taken. "And this thing is INSIDE me? Like Alex was?" He winked dramatically and Alex spluttered and dropped the mush off his spoon.

Star's response was quick. "A tiny part of it, yes. The system itself is on deck 14 below my left ventricular artery. It uses quantum entanglement to speak to each implant, so they can be used anywhere you like."

Shanice sniggered at the shocked reactions of the group. "It's the food that you lot need inside of you, then we can get to work on those repairs. Tick, Tick, Tick people. It's not like we aren't working to a timetable or anything!"

Alex mock saluted her. "Yes, ma'am!" and took another spoonful of the mush and gingerly took a mouthful. "Oh!" He exclaimed. "It tastes ok. Sort of."

Shanice smiled grimly. "Yeah, it's not exactly fried chicken and chips, but it does the job."

"If it is any consolation, we have had greater success in translating INTO your native language than out of it so far, largely thanks to my conversations with Shanice so far." Star mentioned. "At least after the first day. For several hours, all she would say was 'I'm on a spaceship' repeatedly, combined with multiple expletives. My databanks have amassed quite the repertoire of human curse words, including several from different Earth languages. It is quite impressive."

The team laughed gently and Alex and J'Coub slowly tucked in to the food. J'Coub with a mildly distasteful look on his face whilst Shanice continued. "Now, we need a plan of action and thank goodness it's not just me anymore. So far, I have been tending to and repairing some of the biological elements of the Star's body."

"Incredible!. Were you a biologist or something? How on earth did you know where to begin?" Alex asked in wonder.

Shanice snorted. "Hardly. I worked in a call centre whilst trying to get acting work. No, Star mostly told me what to do. Then they kind of helped me learn quicker, I suppose." She looked awkwardly around the room and spread her hands. "The translator device kind of does a bit more that Star said. The information it reads from your mind and then translates and re-implants can actually do a bit more."

"More?" interjected Sorah. "I can't imagine anything more wonderful than this!"

"Yes," said Alex. "What do you mean more?"

Shanice took a breath and grinned at them. "A LOT more. With my permission, Star implanted into my brain the knowledge and skills to be her Medical Officer. It's so weird guys! But I now KNOW how to do these things. It is like I went to a super alien med school in less than 30 minutes. Oh, and Alex, before you start Dr Crushering me, the med officer is also a kind of engineer too since a lot of the ship is biological. That's why that was the only unit I could really take, as it was so urgent."

J'Coub sat forward, letting his spoon drop back into the bowl, his eyes glittering with interest. "And we can reproduce this procedure? With other types of knowledge?"

Star spoke. "We can indeed. In fact, if we want to survive this, it is vital we do so. Some of the limitations imposed upon me by the Vrexen mean that I will always operate best with a crew."

"Bagsy Pilot!" shouted Alex across the table. "I always wanted to fly planes, and a spaceship is WAY better!"

Sorah edged towards the table cautiously. "What is a Bagsy Pilot?"

Shanice smiled as the young woman tentatively joined them at the table. "Oh, it's another Earth saying. It sort of means he is claiming the pilot role if he can."

Star made that unusual chuckling sound. "I am afraid I am quite capable of steering myself through space, Alex. I have been doing it for centuries, after all."

"Oh Arse. I was SO excited for a moment there." Alex grinned anyway.

"Yes, from your elevated neural activity, it was that, or you were about to experience a disruption of electrical activity in your brain. Maybe something missed from your fall from that roof," Star deadpanned.

Shanice laughed loudly, "Oh, Burn. Even the ship has sass. I like it here. Alex, you have got to tell me the roof story."

J'Coub smiled and said, "It's a heroic story. I have your back, Alex."

Alex coughed. "No time! We are on a deadline, remember?" He nodded at J'Coub. "So what do you suggest, Star?"

The ship rippled slightly and continued. "I have formulated a suggestion based on scans of your brain patterns and unique neurological capacities, information recorded by the Vrexian's along with conversations I have overheard. I believe that we have an urgent need for the following positions based on immediate and long-term need. First, we need a technological engineer to complete repairs and improvements to those elements of my structure. I have a solution to this, which is currently not within this room."

"Is this the other being you mentioned?" J'Coub asked curiously.

"Yes." Replied Star simply. Offering no further information. "From the three of you, I will need an Information Officer to assist with navigation and communication. A Tactical Officer to handle any threats we may encounter, including my previous unknown attacker and finally I will need a captain to unify us as a group and to make any decisions where there is dissent among us."

J'Coub interjected. "I assume you have allocated those roles based on your statement around scans? I know I would make a terrible captain. Running the gallery and bar was bad enough. I had to hire people to do all the tedious bits. Drinking wine and talking rich patrons into buying artwork was my speciality."

Alex nodded in agreement. "Even though I was a soldier, I don't think I exactly excelled as one, but if that is what you have calculated, I would be happy to give Tactical a go."

"Indeed." Star responded. "Therefore, I have assigned Information Officer to J'Coub, Tactical Officer to Sorah and Captain to Alex."

Sorah gasped. "But I am not a warrior! I understand so little of this. I only watched the young!"

The bioluminescent lighting along the ceiling glittered in response, and Star continued. "On the contrary, your reflexes and fight-or-flight response are incredibly evolved, Sorah. You protected your young from danger despite the fear that it induced in you. With the right knowledge and skills, you can hone that sense even further. We can even assist with biological and chemical adaptations to manage or even mitigate the worst of your fear whilst still keeping that incredible sense of yours."

"J'Coub. Your adaptability and eloquence mean that you would make an excellent Information and Communications Officer. Along with adaptations unique to your species, that means your mind could also take some extra information stored in our databanks, allowing you a greater understanding of known space."

J'Coub visibly preened at the compliment. "If you say so, Star. It seems that despite my best efforts, I'll be studying some science after all. My parents would be thrilled." He said drily.

"I'm curious why you decided I would be a good captain?" Alex asked.

"Neurologically and personality wise, Shanice would have been my first choice for Captain." Star said. "Unfortunately, it was necessary to implant the medical knowledge into her, as she was the first to awaken and was in one piece. I cannot remove this knowledge or skill without potentially harming the host."

Alex sighed as Shanice desperately tried to cover a snort. "Well, that's a shot to my ego. I guess now I know what it was like for those kids to be picked for a team last at school."

"Actually, the variance in my calculations is incredibly small. The human brain is relatively young and adaptable, so you are both good candidates. Your military training, along with the problem-solving skills you have developed and the manner in which you handled your capture and release have since convinced me you will excel in this role." Star concluded.

"Well, that is a bit more encouraging. So how do we do this?" Alex asked as he finished the last of his food. "Do we all want to do this? Sorah?"

Sorah gripped the edge of the table as if she were holding on for dear life and, for the first time, really looked at each of them and made eye contact. "I…Yes. YES. At home, my people, we adapt or we die. If the food grows sparse in one area, we seek an alternative food source or move our villages. When the weather changes, we fortify our homes. If a tribe member becomes too ill to continue their role, they take on another. I cannot be a silent passenger. The things I have learned they have changed me. I WILL adapt."

"Good for you, girl," Shanice chimed in. "I can't explain it. I am still me, but I just understand all this new stuff and not only do I know it, it feels natural. It isn't like a book has been crammed in my head or anything. I am making new connections and discoveries with the knowledge I have. J'Coub, you can thank me for re-growing and re-attaching your, um, bits. I could actually interpret your biology and work out how best to do everything."

J'Coub's eyes widened, and he instinctively reached down to cover his groin with his hands. "Did you get it all? Nothing is missing, is it? How come everyone seems to have touched my bits?"

Shanice laughed. "All there exactly as it was before, I promise. Even those weird alien ridges."

J'Coub stared in shock and turned to Alex. "You mean you DON'T Have Zytherian ridges? How in the 16 brothers do you procreate?"

Alex looked on in horror. "Why do you always bring the conversation around to sex?"

J'Coub raised a perfectly blue eyebrow. "I suppose it is a defence mechanism."

Alex's gaze softened. "Fair enough, some guys in the army did that too when they were in an unfamiliar..." But J'Coub interrupted him before he could continue.

"A Defence mechanism against BORING conversations!" He retorted and did his weird alien version of Jazz hands again.

The silence in the room was almost deafening.

"On that note," Shanice held a finger in the air. "Who is ready for school?"

5. Meet the crew

Shanice drummed a tuneless rhythm on a datapad in her hands. Each of the budding crew members were arranged on tables in the medical bay, a large chamber a deck down from the bridge. The room was far from the relaxing, welcoming presence that Alex had imagined as they were led there. Bare and sterile mostly, with bubbling tubes of liquid in various shades of blue from a deep navy to the metallic royal that Alex saw on the Sandy haired man's eye socket. In some tubes, indistinct forms spun lazily, coming in and out of focus as they drifted nearer the glass.

He tried desperately not to think what was in those tubes and even harder to ignore the fact the beds that they lay on looked far more like autopsy tables than hospital beds. He closed his eyes and imagined a soft mattress beneath him.

"Now, I'm sorry the tables are cold, but they are originally dissection tables." Shanice's voice rang out cheerfully, shattering his illusions. "The Vrexen were not renowned for their restorative medicine. When I get some time, I promise I will get something more appropriate...At least for most of them."

"Most of them?" Asked J'Coub. "Never mind, I don't want to know..."

"So, are you guys ready? Alex? Sorah? Jakey-Boy?"

"How can I trust a doctor to operate on me when she even butchers my name?" whined J'Coub.

"Do it!" Sorah said, her hands tightly balled into fists and one hoof clicking against the tabletop as her leg shook.

"Ready as I will ever be, Doc." Alex told Shanice.

Shanice nodded to herself. "Then let's get this show on the road." and with a tap of her finger on the pad before her, a gentle hum filled the room.

"Transfer initiated." Star's voice echoed through the pad, sounding oddly tinny from such a small machine.

"How long does this take?" Alex asked Shanice as a strange tingling sensation worked its way from his skull down to his neck.

"Transfer complete." Echoed from the pad.

"All done!" Shanice grinned at their confused faces. "You can get back up now."

"What, no lollipop? No sticker for being a good boy?" Alex joked.

Shanice smiled. Nope! But there are abut 15 dead Vrexen we could do with shoving into an airlock! Star lowered the temperatures in those areas, but they are REALLY starting to stink. Well, stink worse than they did when they were alive and that is saying something!"

Sorah sat up carefully. "It didn't work! I do not feel any different."

Shanice walked over to her and placed a hand on her shoulder, ignoring the slight flinch from the alien woman. "It takes some time for your brain to adjust. Once you get a good sleep, your brain will assimilate the new knowledge. Just you want until you wake up tomorrow morning, Sorah."

Shanice let go of Sorah's shoulder and turned to face the others. "Now, I am serious about those dead Vrexen. Let's get that sorted, then I can show you the facilities and the makeshift dorm I have prepared. Real rooms will have to wait until we have cleared more sections."

Alex sank gratefully into his sleeping mat and wrapped the strange blanket around him. He could hear whispered conversation from the women's side of the room and quiet, melodic snores from J'Coub to his right. He wondered how long it had been since he had slept in a proper bed. Or had actual sleep that hadn't been medically induced. He sniffed his hand subtly and nodded. The third shower seemed to have finally worked on getting rid of the stench from the Vrexen.

He shuddered slightly. Not that he hadn't handled dead bodies before. His brief stint in the army during wartime had popped that particular bubble. Not even was it the sight of his tormentors again that troubled him. It was just that they were SO damn ugly. He persuaded himself that he wasn't being some kind of space racist. After all, he accepted the others quite quickly. It was the wrinkled skin, the wiry hairs that seemed to sprout randomly from their bodies and the almost stereotypically evil looks they had on their faces, even in death.

Alex rolled over, his thoughts racing with the events of the day, and tried to clear his mind as much as possible. The sedative had worn off earlier, and the panic had hit in full force. Sorah had almost fled from them all and he suspected Shanice was still calming her down now. The silver alien had stopped making jokes and his skin was paler than before and Alex was still sweating with nerves.

The lights dimmed gently, as if Star had sensed his need for sleep, and the surrounding blanket warmed slightly. Slowly but surely, he gently drifted to sleep.

As his body gently eased into sleep, his mind, now a fertile ground for the knowledge implanted by Star, began to absorb the training of a captain. The process unfolded in his dreams, a vivid and immersive experience.

In the dreamscape, Alex stood on the bridge of a vast spaceship, much larger and more complex than Star. Panels and screens surrounded him, displaying star charts, technical readouts, and communication feeds. He felt an innate understanding of their purposes, knowledge seeping into his consciousness like water into parched soil.

A crisis alert blared, and the dream shifted. Alex was now commanding a crew through a nebula storm, his commands clear and decisive. Each decision he made felt instinctual, yet backed by a depth of strategic knowledge he hadn't possessed when awake. As the ship entered the nebula, vibrant colours swirled around it, casting an otherworldly glow through the windows. Hues of electric blue, radiant purple, and fiery orange danced like celestial flames, creating a mesmerising spectacle.

However, the danger they were under contrasted with the beauty of the nebula. The unnamed ship shuddered as it encountered turbulent cosmic winds and pockets of dense gas. Each vibration was a reminder of the nebula's raw power. The dream rendered these sensations vividly, with Alex feeling the ship's every movement as if it were an extension of himself.

Lightning-like energy discharges illuminated the nebula, striking near the ship and causing the instruments to flicker and buzz. The sound was a symphony of the cosmos, a blend of low rumbles and high-pitched whistles that resonated through the hull.

In the dream, Alex's senses were heightened; he could feel the charged particles brushing against the ship's shields, each contact sending a shiver down his spine. The navigation through the storm required precision and calm, qualities that the dream was instilling in him.

The scene changed again. Alex was in a large hall, meeting with holographic projections of various alien diplomats of countless shapes and sizes. Navigating the complex interstellar politics with ease, mediating disputes, and forging alliances, Alex felt his diplomatic skills expand, sharpened by Star's implanted training and they felt as natural as his own thoughts.

Amidst these simulations, fragments of historical space battles, legendary captains, and tactical manoeuvres played out like memories. He absorbed lessons from these past events, internalising their strategies and leadership styles.

The dream shifted a final time to a quieter scene. Alex stood in a serene room overlooking a galaxy. Beside him was a figure he recognised as Star, in a more humanoid form (But with a heck of a lot of tentacles, Alex noted). Star spoke of the burdens and joys of leadership, and the importance of empathy, courage, and integrity. These words resonated deeply with Alex, embedding themselves in his psyche.

As dawn approached, the dreamscape faded, but the knowledge and experiences remained integrated into Alex's being.

Alex opened his eyes to the dim light of the early morning aboard Star and, for a jarring moment, expected the next vision. But as he slowly caught up to his reality, a newfound sense of purpose and readiness filled him. The training had been unlike anything he could have imagined, a blend of knowledge and experience directly woven into the fabric of his mind.

One thing remained as usual though, Alex REALLY needed to pee.

The Observation room was already buzzing when Alex finally joined the rest of the team for breakfast. His head was swimming with all the new information he had processed and the short walk here had amazed him constantly as he could now recognise and name various systems and equipment as he walked past.

"Captain on Deck! We are a long way off of finding a good coffee replacement with so many systems still down, but help yourself to a bowl of green slime and a nice mug of hot, thinner green slime!" came Shanice's cheerful voice as she mock saluted him with her spoon, leaving a slight smear of said slime on her face.

"Good Morning Alex of, ah, Alex! Sorry Shanice told me you do not customarily use tribal familial names. I trust you slept well?" said Sorah, whose bowl was already empty. She looked happy this morning, no trace of the nervous young woman from the day before.

"I did thank-you Sorah. Strange dreams, of course, but I imagine that is the same for all of us!" he replied.

"I wouldn't have dropped out of university 3 times if I could have learned like this back then," J'Coub smiled. "This knowledge is amazing. I tried to count the various species I could now name, but I got bored before I finished and invented some cocktails in my head with all the fabulous new alcohols I somehow know from around the galaxy." He darted a sideways glance at his glass of sludge. "I might also volunteer myself as the ship's cook, come to think of it…"

Alex sat down at the table and pulled his bowl towards him.

"I feel I know how to handle almost any situation." Sorah tapped her spoon on her bowl thoughtfully. "At first it was terrifying, seeing all these battles and attacks, but as I realised that the people that were also me, were all capable and knew what they were doing and so I too was capable. The fear. The fear is a wonderful tool. A gift I now know how to use." She smiled at the team and nodded, as if they all understood her lesson.

"Isn't it incredible?" Alex agreed. His face broke into a wide grin, which, combined with his sleep ruffled hair, made him look younger than the 26 years he had. "I know it sounds stupid, but the best part of it is that I don't feel quite so lost anymore. Star, this is a wonderful gift you have given us."

Star's voice echoed from the wall with a hint of pride. "You are more than welcome, Captain. It is thanks to Omni, the ship's computer that we salvaged those memories and simulations and although Omni is still not fully functional again, we both hope that working as a team you four and myself will bring all the parts that have become me back online."

J'Coub rubbed his chin ridge thoughtfully. "Is Omni a thinking being like the rest of us?"

"All Omni does is think Mr J'Coub." Star said wryly. "But not quite in the same way as the rest of us. Omni was created by linking a vast amount of neural material from countless different species with technology to create an incredibly powerful computer. There is a mix of matter and extracted neurons along with entire brains which sit in a nutrient bath within my body. Although little remains of individual personalities within this gestalt, Omni and I have been interlinked for centuries now and I can understand its wishes to a degree and it understands all enquiries and demands." The team looked a little shocked at this full explanation. "But I am still effectively the 'Voice' of Omni and whilst it is in its current state, any conversation we have is insufferably slow and painful."

Sorah stood quickly, her hoofs clacking on the floor as she did so. "Then we will go help Omni this instant!"

Alex choked on his last mouthful of slime at the sudden movement combined with the very 'Hogwarts' way Sorah sounded in that last sentence, but was swiftly spared the embarrassment when Star spoke again.

"Indeed Sorah, it is one of the two most vital tasks and one we will tackle today along with reviving the Engineer. I suggest we split into two teams, with Alex and Sorah retrieving The Engineer and J'Coub and Shanice attending to Omni. This would be a most effective use of your new abilities and your natural talents. Especially since Omni is organic."

"Can you tell us more about the other crew member Star?" Alex asked curiously

A chime sound came from the wall and Star's voice emerged, more muted than before. "I am afraid I must temporarily shut my higher functions down before you proceed any further. You will be fine. I trust you." At which the lights dimmed, and the voice grew silent.

Sorah nodded thoughtfully. "In that case, Alex, I am eager to get started. Star seems to have more delightful bugs to lead the way…"

Alex looked curiously at the dim panel he had come to associate with Star. "That was really odd."

Shanice raised her eyebrows at Alex. "It's happened a few times over the past week. I am guessing it is some kind of automatic response to the damage done throughout the body. I doubt it is anything to worry about." She turned to J'Coub and grinned. "I guess it's you and me then, Silver Balls!" she gestured to J'Coub.

"Silver Balls are fantastic events families on my homeworld throw for their children when their skin tone comes through at 18. I know that won't be what you meant, but it is certainly how I shall take it." J'Coub huffed. "But it would be a pleasure to work with you, madam. Whilst you are shoulder deep in this nutrient bath, I, as Information Officer, will happily direct you."

"You can direct this!" she replied, making a rather obscene gesture.

"Well, it's your middle digit, and it is pointing towards the ceiling. But I believe we are actually heading down towards the core, so I think it is best if you followed me."

Alex sighed as he watched the bickering duo head away, relieved that he was working with the gentle Sorah instead. "Well, talk about a quick breakfast!" He said. "Lets go, Sorah, lead the way." He turned towards her only to find she was already gone and there was only a series of twinkling lights along the floor to lead him away.

6. Omni

Shanice and J'Coub proceeded with care down a sloping corridor. The walls glistened, and the air was noticeably warmer to the senses.

"Star seems to have developed an infection in this area." Shanice noted with concern. "I imagine it may be the same in other areas where there is damage that has gone un-repaired."

J'Coub delicately touched the wall with a hand. "Is it treatable?"

Shanice watched him. Despite his sarcasm and carefree attitude, there was genuine concern in his voice. She wondered again if he was inherently extravagant or if there was a story behind it. "Oh yes, not a problem at all. As soon as we have these two systems online, we will replicate the correct anti-biotics. Star insisted we leave it for now, anyway."

J'Coub nodded, and his face wrinkled in anger. "Star is a good being. It appals me to think how long she has suffered. I only hope the Vrexen suffered when Star poisoned them, and I don't care how that makes me sound."

"It makes you sound like a good man, J'Coub." Shanice patted his shoulder.

J'Coub looked at her in surprise, and a wry grin crossed his face. "Did you know the shoulder is an erogenous zone in my people?" He barked a laugh as Shanice whipped her hand back as if burned.

"I swear J'Coub, I have only known you a day and a half and I somehow suspect if we left you alone in a room, you would get bored and flirt with a chair." She replied, amused.

He appeared thoughtful for a moment. "Interesting. I detest being alone, so I have never had cause to test your theory."

"You don't spend much time alone, huh?"

"Not for a long period of time, no. I have 13 brothers, 11 sisters and 5 people in my parental group, so there wasn't a great deal of opportunity growing up. Since I left home I have averaged around 3 partners at a time, not many really, but the Gallery took up so much of my life!"

"You have relationships with more than one person at a time?" Shanice asked him.

"Oh yes. I know it's not that way amongst many species, but typically we have multiple partners and eventually settle into a large parental unit to raise our children, each contributing to a different aspect of their upbringing and education. That is the other way I disappoint my parents sadly, no desire for children. Practically unheard of on my homeworld. The same reason most of my mates do not stay around very long, either."

"I never wanted kids either. Theres a huge expectation on my world too, that all women want to get married and have children, but even from a young age I just never saw myself wanting that." She breathed as they continued down the damp, humid corridor. "My boyfriend and I argued about it recently, even though I told him from the start. He knew I am Ace and didn't want kids. Arsehole kept pushing it anyway, he probably thinks I've run off with someone else."

"Good Graces! Why would he think you would change your mind? You were honest with him and he expected different from you? He doesn't sound like a very good mate to me, Shanice. Look, my people may be overly forthcoming on emotional matters, me especially, but sacred to every relationship, no matter how many partners, is the foundation of truth and consent. Neither are debatable when pairing with another." J'Coub paused slightly. "I think that although we are very different, we are also alike the four of us, in some ways. I make no apologies for being myself, Shanice, but if I ever offend you, please tell me so I can adjust my behaviour around you."

"J'Coub! I promise you I wasn't offended! Your cheeky sense of humour has really helped lightened the mood. Cheers for telling me more about your people, though."

J'Coub smiled and nodded to Shanice. "I think all four of us have a lot to learn about each other. Sorry Star, all 5. Oh and I assume 6 when the others find this engineer." He halted abruptly as they reached a door in the wall. "Oh, I believe that we have reached our destination."

Shanice eyed the closed door wearily. Just as warm and damp as the rest of this section of the ship, the biological doorway looked swollen shut and blister like welts dotted the left half of the aperture. "Looks like we are going to have to force it open. Care to give me a hand?"

J'Coub reached forward and gripped the thin line down the centre of the door as Shanice did the same. "Ready when you are."

"Now!" Shanice shouted, and the pair grunted in effort as they pulled with all their might. The centre of the door parted with a wet pop and a gust of sour, stale air rushed out. "Keep going," Shanice said through gritted teeth as they slowly peeled the doorway back enough to give space to enter. "There!"

J'Coub wrinkled his nose in distaste. "That smell is disgusting. Are we sure it is safe to go in there?"

"Unfortunately, yes, that's the nutrient gel going stagnant. I need to get the filters working properly first before any of the neural matter deteriorates any further. Then we can work on the connections. But first I need to get IN the tank. There should be a protective suit in there somewhere I can use."

Shanice and J'Coub entered the room, and the sight that greeted them was both awe-inspiring and unsettling.

Dominating the space was the massive vat, about 20 meters high, filled with nutrient fluid. Within it, a complex network of brains and neural matter intertwined with technological components, creating a surreal, organic-technological hybrid. The vat was translucent, allowing them to see the intricate dance of bioluminescent neural pathways pulsating with a rhythmic, eerie glow in the cloudy liquid.

The room itself was vast, with high ceilings that arched above like the interior of a cathedral. Strategically placed workstations and monitoring equipment displayed a myriad of data around the vat, with a constant stream of information flowing in and out of the core.

The screens flickered with readings, graphs, and 3D representations of neural activity, creating a symphony of soft, electronic hums and beeps.

The air was thick with the scent of the nutrient gel, a heavy, almost organic aroma that spoke of life and decay in equal measure. The temperature in the room was warmer than the rest of the ship, contributing to the almost greenhouse-like atmosphere.

Shanice moved towards a console near the vat, her hands hovering over the controls, ready to start the intricate process of reviving and repairing the core. J'Coub, despite his initial discomfort at the smell, looked around in fascination, his eyes taking in the remarkable fusion of living brain tissue and advanced technology.

"This is the heart of Star," Shanice murmured, almost in reverence. "It's here that we'll begin bringing the ship back to herself." She glanced at the walls. Maintenance tools and equipment were neatly arranged, including the Vrexen protective suits that she had known were there. These suits, designed for protecting the nutrient bath from contamination when undergoing maintenance, hung like silent guardians waiting to be utilised.

There were 3 of them, all large and heavy, their copper coloured exterior glittering slightly in the rhythmic waves of light. "Those don't look like they are going to be fun to wear." She sighed. "Help me get one down?"

J'Coub stepped up to help wrangle one of the heavy suits down from the wall. "The Vrexen had no taste whatsoever. Yet another string to their sordid bow." He sniffed in distaste as they lowered the suit to the ground and a pungent whiff of Vrexen seeped from the open neck area. "I am adding quartermastcr to my unofficial duties. I don't know how long we will be aboard for, but we will NOT be slumming it."

Shanice nodded in agreement. "Happy to help you there. I can't wait until we get better accommodation on board and we need to find new clothes or we will stink as bad as those bastards."

"I'm designing us uniforms in my head already! We will look fabulous!" J'Coub smiled. "Right, let's get you into this thing. Do you go straight in the top, do you think?" He fumbled around the next of the suit and tentatively stretched the material. "Ah, here we go." He tapped a small button on the side of the next and to his pleasure, it expanded and the suit's tension dropped and it became loose. "Perfect. Auto adjustable. Quite clever really despite the ugly design and unsavoury aroma." He held the suit open for Shanice. "In you go!"

Shanice stepped into the suit as J'Coub shuffled it up over her body. Once she had wriggled her arms and legs into place, she stood there looking awkward in the loose outfit. "I feel like a kid in her parents' clothes. How do I adjust it back again so that it fits me better?"

"Twist the button on your collar and I believe it will adjust to your measurements." J'Coub took a step back to observe as she did so.

With a twist, the suit adjusted itself to more comfortably fit Shanice's slight frame and after a few minor alterations; she nodded happily. "Now I know this thing has a helmet as well, but can't see one around. Can you see it?"

"Push the same dial in and hold it for a moment and one should appear." J'Coub seemed slightly surprised at the fact the knowledge download was so thorough for him. "Fascinating how our knowledge is so specialised in some areas. It would have been great to have a general information module about the ship itself for everyone. It seem's odd that you don't have immediate access to that knowledge as well."

"I suppose this was more of an immediate 'need to know' situation. My mind is bubbling with medical knowledge. I am not sure how much more they could have crammed in there." Shanice pressed the button on the collar of her suit. Quickly, a framework sprung up around her head and face. Bone spines and crustacean like thin legs gripped her scalp, cheeks and chin and then a thin translucent covering unrolled to encase her head and face completely, sealing tightly to the suit collar. "Oh, that was SO cool!"

J'Coub walked around Shanice and checked the suit as he went. "Impressive." He ran his fingers along the join between helmet and suit. "Looks like the seal is secure. How is the air inside there?"

Shanice gave J'Coub a thumbs up. "Feels good, I can feel some airflow and even the smell seems to be venting out." She moved her arms around experimentally and did a couple of squats. "It's surprisingly comfortable and my mobility isn't anywhere as affected as I thought it would be when we first saw it."

J'Coub looked intrigued. "Hmm, plenty of potential. Now you just need to get up to the top of the vat." He pointed to the huge vat to their left, and they both looked up. "I believe if you step on the circular indentation on the floor, that will raise you to the top of the vat."

"Excellent." Shanice attached the small bag of tools to the waist of the suit and stepped over onto the circular indentation on the floor. As she did, the platform beneath her feet came alive. The surface, which at first glance appeared to be metallic, was actually a densely packed layer of bioluminescent fibres, similar in appearance to muscle tissue. As Shanice reached the centre of the circle and stood still, these fibres contracted rhythmically, like the beating of a heart, causing the platform to rise gently.

The fibres glowed softly, illuminating the platform in a pulsating rhythm of light. Movement was smooth and almost silent, with only a faint hum that resonated softly, like a controlled breath. The platform ascended steadily; the fibres flexing and relaxing in a coordinated manner.

As the lift ascended, the walls of the vat beside them also seemed to react to Shanice's presence. Thin, vein-like conduits running along the vat pulsed with a faint glow, synchronising with the rhythm of the platform's ascent. It was as if the entire chamber was responding to her, working in harmony to facilitate her journey to the top of the vat.

"Feels like I'm being carried up by a barnacle!" Shanice shouted down, amazed at the sensation of the organic lift.

J'Coub watched from below, equally fascinated. "It's extraordinary how this place works. I have seen nothing like it before. Almost disgustingly beautiful. It reminds me of something I would display in the gallery."

Upon reaching the top, the fibres slowly relaxed, allowing the platform to come to a gentle halt. Shanice stepped off, now at the top of the vat, ready to begin her task. The platform, having served its purpose, returned to its original position, the fibres dimming and becoming inert once more.

"OK, I'm here." Shanice yelled down. "If you stand by the monitoring console beneath the tank. All I need you to do is let me know if there are any big spikes on the display there."

"Understood." Came J'Coub's smug voice from within her helmet."Also, just thought I would let you know the translation devices we have implanted also act as communicators if we intend our voices for the recipient to hear. Only within our crew, of course."

Shanice jumped slightly and quickly regained her balance. "Thanks for the timely information, Mr Communications Officer." She replied, quieter this time. "OK, I am looking down into the tank. The filters are at the bottom, so I will have to go all the way in to fix this, trying not to disturb any of the brains. Are you ready?"

J'Coub made an attempt at imitating her thumbs up gesture from earlier, but quickly gave up. "Ready."

Shanice sat at the edge of the liquid and dropped her lower legs into the liquid below. Palms flat on the side, she gently lowered herself down.

Descending into the vat, Shanice felt a knot of tension in her stomach. Encased in her protective suit, she manoeuvred carefully through the murky nutrient fluid, a dense liquid that slightly obscured her vision yet illuminated by the bioluminescent fibres on the walls of the vat.

As she descended, the suspended brains and interwoven technological components became more apparent. They floated in the nutrient fluid, an eerie ballet of organic and synthetic matter. A myriad of fine, glowing tendrils, creating a network that was both fascinating and unsettling, connected with each brain. Shanice moved with deliberate slowness, acutely aware that any contact might disrupt the delicate balance of this bizarre ecosystem.

The brains, varying in size and shape, seemed almost to pulse with a life of their own. Metallic frameworks encased some brains, while others were intertwined with thin, vein-like wires. The sight was mesmerising and navigating through this labyrinth, Shanice focused intently on not touching anything. Guided by the knowledge implanted by Star, she was precise and focused.

Feeling like an intruder in a sacred temple, where every step could have unknown consequences. The deeper she went, the more the sense of isolation and pressure mounted. The surrounding liquid grew denser, and the light from above faded, making her feel as if she were diving into the depths of an unknown ocean.

Finally, she reached the bottom of the vat, where the filtration system was located. It was a large, intricate assembly of tubes and membranes, covered in a fine layer of sediment and algae-like growths. The filter, once a vibrant part of the vat's ecosystem, now looked neglected and clogged.

Shanice's heart raced as she began her work. She knew the importance of getting the filtration system operational; the health of the entire ship depended on it. Every move she made was slow and deliberate, her hands steady despite the adrenaline coursing through her veins.

As she worked, the silence of the vat was all-encompassing, broken only by the sound of her own breathing and the soft hum of her suit. She spoke quietly to J'Coub.

"I'm removing the blockages on the filter now. It also looks like a piece of metal from the deck below has pierced upwards, causing the initial damage, so I will have to remove that."

"Understood." Came J'Coub's calm voice. "You are doing great so far, nothing alarming in any of the readings." His fingers danced elegantly across the diagnostic panel as if this were something he had done countless times before. "Just go steady."

"Steady as a Surgeon. Which, by the way, I totally am now. Maybe if I ever get back to Earth, I could get a leading role in a medical drama?" She mused, only half jokingly. Carefully, Shanice used the cutting tool at her waist to remove the jagged piece of metal and carefully placed it into her pouch. "Ok, the blockage is dealt with. I just need to seal the wound where it came through, then use the regenerator on the biological components."

She carefully replaced the cutting tool and took out the medical regenerator with an artificial instinct. A soft glow lit the end of the device and the tissue around the wound gently grew closed. Once finished, she took a moment to clear some of the dead tissue from around the filter and stood back up. "Done all I can here, ready to ascend. Lights still green?"

As Shanice activated the ascent mechanism, ready to leave the depths of the vat, her relief was short-lived. The moment the filtration system whirred back to life, J'Coub's monitor turned an ominous shade of amber. The sudden reactivation of the system sent a surge of energy throughout the vat, stirring the nutrient fluid into a turbulent spiral.

"Shanice, the readings are changing!" J'Coub's voice crackled through the communicator. "The filter's starting up on its own, and it's causing some instability. Be careful!"

A delicate obstacle course back to the top replaced the gentle ascent Shanice had expected.

The nutrient fluid around her turned into a maelstrom, churning with renewed vigour as the filtration system came back online.

The brains and their connecting tendrils, once floating serenely, now swirled around her in a hazardous dance.

Shanice's heart pounded in her chest. She gripped the sides of her suit, trying to maintain control. Her eyes darted around, searching for a clear path through the swirling organic matter.

Every move had to be calculated to avoid contact with the brains. Any damage could critically endanger the supercomputer.

A large, encased brain loomed directly in her path, spinning towards her with alarming speed. With an agile manoeuvre, she narrowly avoided the collision, feeling the rush of fluid against her suit as she passed by.

"Almost there, Shanice! Just a bit more!" J'Coub's voice was tense but encouraging.

The ascent felt interminable, each second stretched out as she navigated the volatile environment. Another close call came as a cluster of tendrils whipped towards her, and she twisted her body, relying on her instincts and the suit's mobility to evade them.

Finally, after what felt like an eternity, Shanice emerged from the top of the vat.

She gasped for breath. Even though her oxygen supply had been constant, the safety of the surface was a stark contrast to the chaos below.

"I'm out," she managed to say, her voice a mix of exhaustion and relief.

J'Coub let out a sigh that echoed through the communicator. "That was too close. You did it, though. The readings are stabilising, and the filter is operational."

Shanice peeled herself out of the suit, her movements slow and deliberate. The adrenaline was wearing off, leaving her with a profound sense of fatigue. She took a moment and wiped her brow.

As she stepped away from the vat, she couldn't help but look back at the massive container, now calm once more. "J'Coub, when you become the quartermaster-slash-cook, the first thing I need you to make is something alcoholic."

J'Coub nodded in response. "Naturally, it was top of my list anyway. I'm not a barbarian!"

Shanice grinned. "Next thing is the connectors. Let's hope the others are having it easier than we are."

7. The Engineer

Sorah strode purposefully down through what passed as the engine room on Star, with Alex rushing to keep up. The room was huge, with high, arched ceilings and walls that pulsated gently, echoing the rhythm of a living organism. The organic components of the room had a fluid, almost muscular texture, seamlessly integrated with the ship's structure.

The core of Star's propulsion system was an astonishing sight. At the centre of the room stood a massive, translucent organ, resembling a giant heart, rhythmically contracting and expanding. This was Star's original method of propulsion, a biological engine capable of generating powerful thrust through the manipulation of space-time fabric. It worked on the principle of organic manipulation of energy fields, a natural ability of Star's species to bend and warp space, allowing for travel at considerable speeds.

A network of vein-like conduits connected the organ, spreading out across the room and pulsating with a luminescent energy. These conduits carried the energy generated by the organ to various parts of the ship, ensuring efficient distribution of power. If he stared long enough, Alex could almost see where they had carved out the flesh around the organ and pinned the veins back to the ceiling and walls, and he felt sickened once again at the irreversible damage done to their new friend.

Naturally, the Vrexen, in their quest to exploit Star's abilities, had made significant technological modifications. Surrounding the organic engine were arrays of mechanical devices and control panels, integrated somewhat intrusively into Star's viscera, designed to enhance and control the engine's capabilities, pushing it beyond its natural limits for faster and more precise travel.

One of the most noticeable additions was a series of large, crystalline structures positioned around the organic engine. They glowed with an intense light, pulsing in sync with the engine's rhythm. Alex knew from memory that these crystals were quantum resonance amplifiers, a Vrexen technology that harnessed and amplified the energy produced by the organic engine, allowing for more powerful propulsion and the ability to make controlled jumps through space.

Despite the technological enhancements, the room maintained a balance between the organic and mechanical, a testament to the Vrexen's understanding of Star's unique physiology. However, there was a sense of strain in the air, as if the organic parts were under constant pressure from the unnatural additions. Carved into the bone along the wall was a crude representation of a Vrexen head, looking halfway between graffiti and an idol. Sorah snorted disdainfully. "I wonder what J'Coub would make of their 'art'."

As Alex and Sorah moved through the room, they could feel the hum of energy and the subtle vibration of the ship's power. "We need to pass through here and into the next section according to Star's instructions." Sorah said whilst consulting her datapad. "This would be much easier if Star were to guide us in real time."

Alex finally caught up to Sorah, slightly breathless and red in the face but thrilled that there was no pain from his once ravaged back. "Hey, who knew our spaceship needed to nap? At least with us here to help, Star can focus on getting some rest so they can heal as much as possible."

"I understand, but I dislike the fact that whilst we are all otherwise occupied and Star is effectively out of service, nobody is on watch. Star was attacked a week ago by a mysterious assailant and we do not know if they have the capabilities to track us." Sorah stopped briefly and looked to see if Alex was listening to her. She nodded at him and continued on. "We need to return to monitoring duty, check for hull damage, and get our weapons systems back online as quickly as possible."

Alex was stunned by the change in Sorah from when he had initially met her. "I agree Sorah. Naturally, we will also need to balance that with our basic needs and ensure that we can reverse any other damage that poses a major risk to Star. I'm impressed at how easily you have adjusted to the Tactical Officer role." He felt she had grown into her position on the ship and adapted to her role far quicker than he had. Despite the new knowledge in his head, he had felt no actual change in his personality or confidence levels like Sorah obviously had.

Sorah grimaced slightly as they passed the halfway point of the room. "My mind is going over all the threats we may face, Alex, and then coming up with solutions or counter-attacks. Around and around, these thoughts go. I thought at first it was like the anxiety I suffered from back on my homeworld, but instead, each solution gives me strength. I not only think about these things, but I have an overwhelming urge to DO. It is exhilarating to be true."

She looked at Alex again and slowed her pace slightly, realising that her species was naturally much faster than a human. "I want to explore and repair the weapon systems, then I want to upgrade them if need be. Access to the armoury is vital, so I can catalogue and clean the weaponry there. I have already laid out plans for training sessions for the team and counter arguments for J'Coub's attempts to make excuses not to do them." She smiled at him briefly.

"I want to utilise some drones and ships that I know are in the hangar and see what defensive modifications I can make to them. I want us to be SAFE Alex. Star needs to feel like she never needs to worry about being subjugated again. I never want to go back to being the person I was." She stopped again and looked Alex in the eye, her face set in a determined look. "And I want to make absolutely sure that the Vrexen do not take one more person from their homeworld and subject them to the torture that we have faced."

Alex stopped too and smiled up at Sorah, impressed. "Regroup, Rebuild, Revenge. Sounds like a plan to me, Sorah. But let's make sure we are in the best possible place before we act. I'm betting you could use an engineer when fixing up those weapons."

"I was not suggesting otherwise, Captain, merely hoping that we can do this quickly. Star said that we would find our missing crew member in stasis cell 8, but she did not give us any other information on what to expect, which seems unlike our host so far."

Alex nodded. "I agree. It seems strange. Star either won't say more about them or can't say more about them. I suspect that it's the latter and Star has some kind of lock still on her systems or some gaps in her memory that are preventing her from saying any more. It seemed more than just needing to shut down for a while to me. She hasn't done anything to make me think we can't trust her, but we should still proceed carefully."

Sorah sighed. "I am glad I am not the only one that finds it strange. Star has also not been forthcoming when I questioned her about the weapons systems on board. The memory download is quite generic and I still have only rudimentary knowledge of this ship's capabilities."

"It's the same with the Captain's download I got. In the dreams I Captained hundreds of ships, but never Star, even though she appeared in my dream in a smaller form." Alex agreed sadly. "But whatever is waiting for us, it is in the next room, so I suggest we should be on guard."

Sorah reached down and pulled a device from her waist. "I took this from one of the Vrexen when we were moving the bodies. Star seems to have provided Shanice with medical tools, but no weapons for me. I suspect they may still be stored in the armoury which is inaccessible for now, but this appears to deliver electrical discharges, so it will do for the time being." The pair reached the doorway, which hung limply open, with only darkness inside awaiting them.

"This area only has emergency power," Sorah stated warily as she moved to take position to the right of the doorway. "How do you wish to proceed, Captain?"

Alex instinctively took position to the left of the doorway, using the wall as cover. He had grabbed a long piece of bone that had fractured from the wall and wielded it in his right hand as a makeshift weapon. "I have an idea. One moment." Alex turned his head back into the room and looked towards the glittering trail of light bugs that had led them here. There was enough light from the glowing crystals around the engine to light the space adequately. "Hey, Glowbugs. I am hoping you can understand me here. Would you please move into the next room and spread out as evenly as possible to illuminate the room?"

For a moment the bugs did nothing, but then a dim pulse shivered through the pathway and the tiny creatures marched in a double file into the room ahead, spreading out as they did so and bringing a soft glow to the room ahead.

"I'm so glad that worked." Alex sighed with relief. "Now, let's see what we are facing."

Sorah steeled herself for a moment and risked a quick glance into the other room, taking stock of what lay ahead before returning to position. "Alex, from what I can see, this is some kind of laboratory and storage area combined. There are cells around the room which look to contain organic remains. It looks's safe to enter, but I fear we may be too late."

"Alex nodded to her. On three, I will enter the room and you follow me and provide cover if necessary, as you have the long-range weapon. One, Two…Three!"

Alex and Sorah moved swiftly into the room, the pair naturally working together as a unit. As Alex examined the space, a chill ran down his spine.

"All clear." Said Sorah and then stopped in her tracks. The hairs on her neck and arms raised slightly as the sight before them became clear.

Along one wall of the room, cell after cell stood starkly against the hull. Each one is no more that 3 feet across. The doorways shimmered with an almost imperceptible field designed to keep the occupants inside, and hard chitin walls separated the tiny rooms. Neatly labelled shelving and crates occupied the other walls, reaching from floor to ceiling, with some enclosed in their own fields. A ridge of what looked like a spine snaked out from the floor along the centre of the room, raising to around waist height at the centre before dipping into the floor again.

They had levelled the bone in the centre of the room off to create what looked like a long workbench with various items strewn across it, including a pungent mess of what was once some poor creature's limb.

Alex moved cautiously towards the cells. "This place has awful vibes to it. Let's find cell 8." There was no motion from any of the cells as they passed them, whatever was inside each one held in stasis or long since perished. Alex stopped at their destination.

"Cell 8. Looks like we are too late. There is nothing inside but a pile of dust. Whatever was here seems to have died a long time ago." Sorah remarked. She looked more relaxed than before, but still held her weapon at the ready.

Something tickled at the back of Alex's mind, and he held up a hand. "Wait. I think I know what's going on here, but I'm not sure you are going to like it."

Sorah looked at the pile of dust and back to Alex. "Oh great. More things for me to dislike. What is your evaluation?"

"I think what we have here is inert nanotechnology. On one ship in my vision, the crew were delivering experimental medical technology utilising prototype nanites. In storage, they looked a lot like this." He peered closer at the enormous pile. "They activated the nanites with an electrical pulse. If we want to see what this stuff does, we'll need to drop the field and hit it with a low charge from your stunner."

"IF we want to see what it does. It could do anything Alex. What kind of technology would the Vrexen keep inert and in stasis and not utilise on board the ship?"

"Star seems to think it's related to our engineer. So it may be a tool or a drone of some kind. Look, there is only one way to find out. I will drop the stasis field for a few seconds and you hit it with a low charge. Then I'll raise the shield again and we can safely see what it is. Sound good?"

Sorah thought for a moment and nodded. Her horns glittered slightly in the dim light from the bugs. "Do it"

Alex stepped towards a panel on the side of the cell, and his fingers danced across the screen. "NOW!"

Sorah took aim and fired a bolt of electricity from the weapon before the shield shimmered into life again. The pair stood expectantly watching the pile of dust, but nothing happened.

Alex reached for the screen again. "Another time, amp up the charge by 25%. And, now!"

Sorah repeated the blast, the bolt of electricity brighter than before and giving an audible buzz this time. The screen in place once more, they watched intently as the pile of dust rippled, the uppermost section tumbling back towards the floor disturbed by the weapon's power, then stilled again.

Alex turned to Sorah. Once more I think, full power this time. Whatever it is, it looks completely drained of power. He once again lowered the shield, and Sorah fired again.

This time, the weapon produced a loud buzz as a long streak of lightning arced across the space and danced around the pile. As the shield came into place once more, they watched as the dust sparked and sizzled and rolled into itself and formed a shape. Slowly, the dust packed down harder and solidified bit by bit until it formed an egg shape about the size of a rugby ball to Alex's eyes. The shape rocked gently back and forth on the floor of the cell until blue lights lit the sides.

"What is it?" Sorah asked incredulously. But as Sorah spoke, the egg righted itself until it balanced on one of its points and gently rose into the air. It settled into a hover in front of their heads.

The surface of the object pulsated with a rhythmic blue glow. Without warning, it emitted a series of rapid beeps and mechanical whirs, propelling itself through the stasis field with ease and towards the shelves laden with assorted materials and equipment.

"Get back!" Sorah shouted to Alex. "Take cover quickly."

They both crouched down behind the large bone table, weapons gripped tightly as they observed the strange object. It spun languidly in place as a bright blue beam of light emanated from it and passed over the space.

"It's scanning the room," Alex observed, his voice tinged with nerves and curiosity.

The thing moved with precision, extending small, multi-limbed appendages to deftly pick and put back items from the shelves. Every so often, it seemed to find something significant. A unique pattern of sounds - a language of beeps, buzzes, and clicks that seemed to almost have a structure accompanied each selection. They watched warily as it took an item and the glittering dust like nanotechnology, enveloped it, shaping it and attaching it to itself.

Sorah watched intently. "It's building something... or rather, modifying itself," she noted, a sense of awe in her voice.

In a flurry of mechanical grace, the thing began to adapt its form. It attached lightweight but sturdy limbs that could extend and retract, integrating tools and sensors as needed. The assembly process was both efficient and mesmerising, with components floating in the air and attaching to the core seamlessly under its guidance.

The sounds it emitted grew more complex, light beeps and chittering when it seemed to attach something it liked and low rumbles when it placed something back again. Within moments, it had transformed itself into a floating sphere, the blue core glowing at the centre. What looked like multiple short limbs dangled beneath it and four more sprung from its side like arms.

Once its self-modification was complete, the thing floated towards Alex and Sorah. Though it lacked a traditional face, its central core flickered with lights, suggesting a form of active engagement. It hovered before them and chirped out a brief tune, and waved its limbs gently in the air. To Sorah's surprise, Alex stood.

"It's not just a machine; it's like... it's thinking, adapting," Alex said, stepping forward. "Hello there. I'm Alex, and this is Sorah. You must be The Engineer, right?"

Responding to Alex's voice, The Engineer emitted a series of harmonious tones and extended one of its limbs in a gesture of acknowledgment. Interpreting this as a greeting, Sorah rose from her hiding place and gently reached out to touch the limb, smiling at the interaction.

Intrigued by its new environment, The Engineer emitted a sequence of excited tones and began to move around, its sensors scanning and assessing the room more fully. It occasionally paused, produced a series of sounds, and then resumed its exploration.

"We should keep up with it," suggested Alex. "It might be trying to assess the ship's condition, or it could need our help with something."

"Or it could be deciding where best to dissect us?" Sorah deadpanned.

Alex shrugged in response. "Potato Poh-Tah-Toh."

8. Problem Solving

Alex and Sorah followed The Engineer as it floated eagerly into the engine room, whistling excitedly. As they all entered the cavernous space, the bug lights followed them, arranging themselves neatly back into their original lines. The Engineer paused briefly to inspect them flying low to the ground and beeping in satisfaction before rising to scan this room too. It hovered gently at the giant engine in the centre, orbiting the powerful device and its unintelligible chattering lowering in tone to an almost sad, dirge like moan.

"I know." Alex said gently to the robot. "The entire ship is a living being, captured and experimented on until the Vrexen slowly enslaved it and made it into a spacecraft. Her name is Star."

The Engineer paused and sank a little lower in the air, then gently hovered over to alex and extended one of its arms onto the side of Alex's head.

"What is it doing?" Sorak asked cautiously.

"I think it's checking to see what I am?" Alex replied and made sure he stood very still indeed. The Engineer spun slowly and the scanner light gently swept across Alex. The robot chirped and lightly tapped Alex on the side of his head, then tilted slightly in the air with a questioning aura about it..

"I think that is where the translator is installed." Sorah observed. Alex noticed she had finally sheathed her weapon and her posture was slightly more relaxed now.

Understanding crossed Alex's face. "Oh, no. Star provided this so myself and the other crew could understand each other. The Vrexen didn't do this to me. Star healed me from the damage they did."

The Engineer chirped in understanding.

"Star needs us to help repair the damage done to her. She gave each of us knowledge to help heal her, but half of her body is technological and that level of knowledge either wasn't available to her or was lost in the attack." Sorah explained. "Star pointed us towards you, hoping you could help, but didn't tell us anything about you, so I apologise if we were overly wary."

The Engineer rotated to face Sorah and inclined its body to her as if thanking her, then turned away and began following the lights with purpose. Moving quickly, it reached the door before stopping and gesturing to them with two of its appendages indicating for them to follow it. Alex and Sorah briefly made eye contact with each other and followed their new crew member down the corridor.

The Engineer gracefully floated down the corridor, lazily spinning as it did. The blue beam of its scanner reflecting off the walls as it went. Occasionally it would swoop down to investigate a random piece of wall or an access panel, chirping to itself as it did so until finally they returned to the bridge. The engineer let out a low whistle as they entered the room, its scanning beam brightening as it swept across the space with intensity. Excitedly, it inspected the holographic table and then moved to the various stations spaced around the bridge, pausing at the Captain's chair stationed next to the shuttered viewscreen.

"Star, we are here with The Engineer." Alex reported to the room. "Star?" There was no response.

"Maybe Star is still asleep?" Sorah suggested, nodding towards the living section of wall that she had come to associate with Star. At her gesture, The Engineer whizzed towards the wall and began scanning it with intensity. A series of furious clicks and beeps of varying tones emanated from the small being and, without warning, one of its extremities extended violently through the skin of the wall.

"Engineer! That's Star's skin, where she speaks to us from. Please be very careful," Sorah shouted.

The strange being waved another extremity at Sorah as if in irritation and then roughly pulled its arm out of the wall, clutching a wet cube of technology that he had ripped out from behind the skin. Some of the strange sap like fluid dripped from the wound, fresh and bright, unlike the dried fluids from Star's earlier wounds. The Engineer examined the cube briefly and then threw it violently onto the floor. As he did so, the bioluminescence behind the wall flickered into dim life again.

"Old friend!" Star's voice was slow and warm. "I am so happy to see you again. Did they hurt you?"

The Engineer let out a string of complex noises as it span wildly in place.

"Then I at least am pleased that you do not remember." Star Said. "I must also express gratitude to you, Alex, and Sorah. Thank you for freeing my friend."

"He took us quite by surprise, Star! A heads up would have been nice, but I'm glad that he's here. He is amazing."

Star paused briefly. "My apologies. The Vrexen had installed several inhibitors around my body, one on each neural cortex. Two were damaged during the attack, essentially freeing me. Shanice has removed one for me. I have dealt with four others, but this one prevented me from accessing classified projects, weapons, or any information considered dangerous by the Vrexen." Star continued. "My friend was considered a classified threat and stored in a stasis cell. I could point the way, but not actively talk about him or assist more than I did."

The Engineer chirped and then drifted over to one of the crew stations on the wall. Extruding some equipment from his body, he began to delicately repair the panel.

"I appreciate that Engineer." Star said. "Alex, Sorah, he will be otherwise engaged for quite some time now. He is never happy unless he is working."

"I'm not going to complain about someone fixing things around here, in fact…" but before Alex was finished, Shanice and J'Coub interrupted them returning to the Bridge.

"WHOA, what is THAT?" Shanice remarked in awe. "We have a robot? Guys, we have a ROBOT!"

Sorah stood by The Engineer, watching it work with fascination. "His name is The Engineer."

"He's so cool." Shanice was practically fawning over him now as the being waved an arm towards her as he worked. "Is he a repair drone or something?"

Star's lights dimmed slightly then flared an orange colour. "He is a fully sentient AI being Shanice. Very few of his kind have ever been seen, but he and I have encountered each other many times over the centuries. It is rare for his race to leave their homeworld, but my friend here has an insatiable curiosity that cannot be contained." The glow from Star settled into a warm yellow. "He knew me from before I was taken. We would encounter each other every 100 years or so and would exchange conversation and information, as much as I could at the time. I hadn't seen him since I was captured, but when our paths crossed again about 10 years ago, he tried to free me. In vain. Since then, he has been a 'specimen' for the Vrexen to study, held dormant and my sensors in that area cut off. I am only glad he was still there."

Shanice and J'Coub seated themselves wearily at the central console. J'Coub gracelessly dumped an armful of the protective suit, all deactivated and loose, onto the chair next to him. He turned and nodded to The Engineer. "Welcome to the crew. I brought a spare suit, but it looks like you will be just fine without one." He inclined his head. "I am J'Coub, information officer and the loud one over there is Shanice, Medical Officer, pleased to meet you." J'Coub stuck out his hand in welcome.

The Engineer turned and ran its scanner over them both and then extended a gripper arm and gently shook J'Coub's hand and then waved cheerily at Shanice. The machine then performed what suspiciously looked like a mock salute, burbling and beeping away as he did so before running his scanner over the pile of suits and then returning to his work.

J'Coub "Finally someone with manners aboard this ship!" J'Coub said with a wry grin. "It looks like you two were successful in your mission. Happy to report that Shanice has done a great job of fixing Omni, ably supported by yours truly."

Shanice chimed in, "Yeah, it was touch and go for a while, but we repaired Omni's connections and the nutrient bath is clearing up nicely. Star, how are the connections to your end?"

"I can confirm that I have re-established full connection to Omni now and am compiling a thorough list of internal and external damage. Transferring to your pads now."

Alex nodded and checked the pad in his hand. "Ok crew. Let's take 5, then get to work. Engineer, you do what you need to do. Shanice, same with you but the biological elements, Sorah, weapons' systems naturally. I will take the bridge and engineering and J'Coub if you make sure comms and scanners are active?"

"Yes Captain, I would also like to run inventory in the Cargo Bay and stores and make sure we have enough edible food as well as investigate the facilities if that is ok with you?" the silver alien asked.

Alex nodded to him and faced the rest of the team. "Let's eat and start the hard work then!"

9. Montage

The Corridors

The Engineer glides through the dimly lit corridors of Star, its blue core casting a soft glow. It pauses at irregular intervals, extending its thin limbs to interface with panels and wiring. The limbs, tipped with what seemed like an ever changing variety of tools, move with swift precision, soldering wires and recalibrating circuits. The ship's internal lighting gradually brightens, humming back to life section by section.

Weapons bay 4

Sorah's arms are covered in grease, the fine hair on them matted and filthy. She was elbow deep in the internal components of one of the massive rail guns attached to the ship. Braced into the machine and body tensed, she raised one hoof and slammed it down into the twisted bracing that held the weapon in place again and again until she let out a satisfied huff.

The Engine Room

In the pulsating heart of the ship, The Engineer hovers around the massive, organic engine. It delicately attaches new conduits, integrating them seamlessly with the existing network. A series of satisfied beeps follow each attachment, as the energy flow stabilises, strengthening the ship's power. He reaches out with one metal claw and gently strokes his work.

The Bridge

Panels, newly repaired, shine with information around the Bridge. Alex mutters to himself as he goes over to each one to calibrate them for the mixed crew's best usage. He taps a button on his pad. "Captain's Log…Uh, no, that feels weird…Note to Self. We need seats at each station for the crew. Seems like The Vrexen operated on short rotations and I want my team to be comfortable if we ever have to spend extended periods up here. All stations are up and running fine, but some data is still not coming through from external sensors that are yet to be repaired."

Alex looked over at the Captain's chair then quickly scanned the room to see if anyone was coming. Once he had ascertained he was alone, Alex ran his hands over the back of the seat before reverently sitting down.

A huge grin broke out over his face.

The Hull

Outside in the vastness of space, The Engineer emerges from an airlock, manoeuvring gracefully along the ship's hull, inspecting for damage. Metallic scales neatly fitted over each other covered the vast hull of the ship, providing a flexible and resilient covering for Star.

Finding a breach, He extends an arm, deploying a patch that melds perfectly with the hull material, sealing the gap. Lights blinked rhythmically in his core, signalling a job well done. Spinning back away from the hull, scanning beam widening and small boosters firing intermittently to keep him steady, Star's full body came into view. The immense oval body glimmered in his beam as her scales reflected light back at him. Towards her head, three large ports covered in a transparent material faced forward. Once Star's eyes, the central port was located where the bridge now stood. Shutters visible where the glass like dome had shattered. Her other eyes had long since been converted into sensor arrays and various instruments and appendages were visible around the brutal damage left from the unknown attackers.

The engineer's lights dimmed as it took in the horrific mutilations inflicted on his friend. His species, known for continually adapting and improving their bodies and environment, understood that this was not always the case for others. Slowly, he drifted back along the hull. She was missing the two long feeding arms that had once sat below her eyes. Now, not even a scar remained.

He continued towards the back of the ship, where her massive tentacles drifted in a tight spiral behind her. Of varying lengths and covered in those same scales as her hull, they were a sight to behold. His scans confirmed they had taken less damage than the rest of the hull and needed only minimum repairs. He took a moment to himself and then continued repairing the damage to the hull.

Observation Lounge/Newly designated Mess Hall

"Try the red one." J'Coub insisted to the crew.

The Engineer hovered by the table and subtly scanned the food J'Coub had prepared for the team. He made a low dismissive buzz and floated off the Bridge.

Sorah poked the round, red sphere dubiously. "What is it?"

J'Coub smiled proudly. "Oh, it's all created from the same base materiel as the green slime we had, so it is essentially nutritionally complete, but I have experimented with adding flavour and texture to make it more palatable for us. Give it a go."

Shanice stabbed a fork into one sphere and bravely popped a whole one into her mouth. Biting down carefully, she chewed slowly and her face ran through a variety of expressions in a short space of time before she leaned forward and unceremoniously spat the mush back onto the plate.

"um." She paused for a moment and looked at J'Coub apologetically. "Sorry. I am not sure if our palates are similar. That just tastes metallic to me." She shrugged in apology as Alex and Sorah surreptitiously pushed their bowls away.

J'Coub looked nonplussed. "Oh, I hadn't tried it myself. After version five, I felt rather full. AH well, next time!"

Environmental

Shanice sat back and wiped the sweat from her brow. She had been working tirelessly for the last few days on regenerating as much damaged tissue around the ship. Doors now worked smoothly, scarred walls were now smooth and healthy looking. Today she was tackling the environmental systems on the port side of the ship.

The systems were not too badly damaged from the attack, but looked like they had been neglected for a long time. It also showed some deterioration from whatever biological agent that Star had released through the ship to kill the Vrexen.

Once she fixed that, she needed to ensure that the atmosphere being generated was not just breathable for the new crew as it currently was, but truly optimised for them.

She had slept well last night in her new quarters that she shared with Sorah. J'Coub had somehow cleared two large rooms for them all to share with hygiene facilities between rooms for the entire crew to use. Each room had bunk beds in the centre, sectioned off with an S-shaped divider so that they each had privacy, the bottom bunk had the port side of the room and the top bunk the starboard and a shared space towards the stern. It was enough that they had privacy, but none of the four were ready to be fully alone in this strange new situation.

The Engineer had naturally claimed a spot in Engineering and the room looked different every time one of the team passed by, constantly being re-made in the strange robot's quest for perfection.

Shanice pulled herself up once again and set to work, murmuring to herself as she did. "I'm on a fucking spaceship!"

Cargo Bay

"J'Coub, are you in here?" Sorah asked loudly as she entered the large Cargo Bay. Boxes and crates neatly stacked around the space formed a maze of stored equipment and supplies. She could see colourful markings on the crates where she assumed J'Coub had attempted to label and sort the contents.

"Just round the other side!" came the familiar, lilting tones of the silver man.

Sorah continued walking around the space, marvelling as she saw a row of tables with various projects strewn across them. One contained a makeshift still, an obvious attempt to brew alcohol for the team. Another had two of the protective suits on them, along with bolts of fabric and material that he had scrounged up from somewhere.

Sorah turned the corner to where J'Coub's voice had come from and her senses instantly flared up on alert. She unholstered the new pistol that she had found in the armoury and aimed ahead. "J'Coub, stay perfectly still and do not panic. There are unknown entities just behind you."

J'Coub glanced behind him and looked at the four small creatures behind him. He then turned back to Sorah. "Wait, STOP!" He cried. "They are harmless, I promise."

Sorah raised an eyebrow at him, but did not lower the weapon. "What are they and how did they get on the ship?"

She gestured towards the bizarre crab like beings that were now huddled together, clacking their claws at her.

J'Coub reached down and petted one crab gently. At his touch, the little thing's legs danced beneath it in pleasure. "They are essentially Star's maintenance crew. Or what's left of them. There used to be hundreds of them, but only around eleven remain. I think they have some kind of symbiotic relationship with her, from what I can tell." He reached down and picked up another crab, flipping it onto its back and scratching the hard chitin on its stomach.

Sorah finally lowered her weapon. "I see. And you didn't think of informing the rest of us about this?"

J'Coub held one creature close to his body protectively. "Absolutely not! You would have had one of them down a greasy gun hole quicker than you could say hello!" He shrieked in horror. "Besides, they seem quite fond of me and have been a great help in tasting some of the food creations I have worked on."

Sorah shook her head. "I'm not after your pets, don't worry. It's on your head if they chew through some wiring somewhere."

J'Coub idly rubbed the head of the creature. "Don't worry Tiny, I won't let the nasty Goat Lady get you."

The Bridge

Back on the bridge, The Engineer interacts with the holographic table, projecting schematics and ship diagnostics to Alex, who marvelled at the detailed blueprints and the rapid progress in repairs.

"Great work!" Alex said, as he appraised the latest reports. "Looks like things are coming along nicely. But what are these designs down here?" He pointed towards a section on the lower part of the schematic.

Star's voice chimed in, "I said no, friend. He thinks I would look good with multiple manipulator arms around my hull, but I do not feel that this is necessary."

The Engineer beeped in protest and span his body around waving his various arms around.

"Yes, you look great." Star said. "But I only want you to replace my original frontal tentacles, please. They are what I miss most from before my transformation."

The Engineer buzzed in distaste

"Best do what the lady says, buddy." Alex smiled at the floating droid.

The Medical Bay

In the medical bay, The Engineer assists Shanice in remodelling the equipment to make the space more comfortable, sterile and fit for purpose. Shanice was checking the status of the four stasis pods that they had brought up from their previous prison. Between them, they had refurbished and upgraded the pods into emergency medical suites. The Engineer and Shanice had greatly improved on their capacity for stasis, delivery of pharmaceutics, and surgery.

Now looking sleek with a comfortable padded interior, they had a much less ominous air around them. While The Engineer worked on upgrading the diagnostics table in the centre of the room, Shanice moved on to check some of the biological tools. In a large tank against one wall, she dropped a food package inside. Thousands of tiny ant-like creatures rallied into action, sending organised wave after wave of drones to dissect, gather, and deliver the food to their nest. Fascinated by watching them work, Shanice sat entranced and began humming tunelessly.

At the centre of the room, The Engineer paused in its work. Then, ever so quietly, began beeping and humming along with the tune.

The Mess Hall

J'Coub gestured towards the bowl in the centre of the table with a flourish. "Esteemed guests, I present to you.." He paused dramatically. "Version 48! I am confident this one will stay on the menu."

Sorah and Alex sat still and looked expectantly at Shanice.

"What?" she asked, looking slightly affronted.

Alex at least had the grace to blush slightly. "You ALWAYS go first. It's like your brain erases the trauma of the previous dish each time and you never get sick. It's like your superpower."

Shanice laughed. "Listen, my grandma used to cook chicken foot in stew pea at least once a month back home. I hated it as a kid, but the verbal beating you would get if you didn't eat it, well let's just say I have never been afraid to try new things since." She smiled fondly at the memory of those loud, boisterous family meals at home and church, then grabbed her spoon. "Fine, you pathetic lot. J'Coub, at least tell me you tried this one?"

J'Coub nodded eagerly. "I have indeed. A bit bland for my personal tastes, but I think this is the one that will work for all our palates. Once I have a few more of these staples, I can work on species specific flavours."

Shanice held up her spoon. A delicate yellow cube wobbled slightly as she raised it up in a mock toast. "Bottoms up!" She took a tiny sniff of the food and then popped it straight into her mouth and chewed.

"Well?" Alex asked almost immediately. Shanice raised a single finger in the air.

"How is it?" Sorah added, leaning forward in her seat. Shanice raised a second finger as she swallowed.

Blue light swept across Shanice's face as the engineer scanned her, a querying buzz coming from him.

"J'Coub." Shanice turned to face him. "That is 100%, not bad."

J'Coub's face lit up as if he had just received the highest praise, then he turned to Alex and Sorah expectantly.

Sorah took her spoon and cautiously selected a small portion to taste as Alex followed a second or two later. "Oh! This reminds me of a fruit we have growing near my village. " Sorah smiled. "It's not exactly the same, but it very much reminds me of it."

J'Coub preened. "Good food should always remind you of something from your past. I am glad you like it. Alex?"

Alex nodded to him, swallowing the mouthful he had taken and reaching for more. "Mate, this is good. Sort of like a smooth orange ice-cream, but not cold if that makes sense. I'll definitely eat it again."

"Excellent! Now, tell me more about this ice-cream and why the orange colour is so important…"

The Sensor Array

Hovering near Star's sensor array, The Engineer works to recalibrate the damaged equipment. Tiny tools emerge from its limbs, twisting and turning with meticulous care as he worked to make the sensors fully operational again.

Delicately, he repairs the sensors and adds back in some of Star's original optic nerves that Shanice had re-grown in the lab. He had already done so in the other scanner bay and added some back on the central view-screen. Now he just needed to finish this section, re-glaze the protective dome and Star would be able to see clearly again with her natural vision. Long conversations with Omni and some sedative from Shanice helped ensure that Star wouldn't be overwhelmed with the duelling senses.

The array realigns, and a burst of data flows back to the ship's systems, illuminating Star's navigation screens with new information. Slowly, the shutter over the central eye opens and the crew cheers from within.

Everywhere

Star gently stretched, causing a minute ripple through the ship. Not only was she healed from her recent injuries, but the team had worked hard to remove as many unnecessary adaptations as possible. There was no going back for Star now. Too much of her was lost or changed, and most of her systems now relied on the changes The Vrexen had made. But the small freedoms the team had given her felt good.

For the first time since her blind jump to escape from the attack, Star gently extended her tentacles behind her, uncoiling them and allowing them to float free behind her. The sensation was exquisite and she couldn't resist moving forward a bit in space.

With her original vision restored, she looked at the system she had blindly jumped to. It was uninhabited and full of dense clouds of ice particles and dust. Whether planets never formed or some unknown catastrophe pulverised them, the entire area now comprised a labyrinth of cold, misty debris that effectively covered any ships searching for their thermal heat signature.

But for Star, this was a thing of beauty and every rock and swirl caused a swell of emotion within her.. Cautiously she extended her two new front arms that The Engineer and Shanice had helped create for her. Before the change, she had used them for feeding and she imagined reaching out for rocks and asteroids to sort and filter. She missed eating. It had been hundreds of years since she last needed to eat, but seeing her crew experimenting with food had made her feel wistful for those days.

She reached forward and ran them through a dense cloud of ice and rock. It felt different from what she remembered, but she felt! Ice cold granules gently bounced off of her arms, translating the sensations via the sensors to her brain. She casually gripped a rock and pulled it towards her, marvelling at the small craters and bumps that she felt along the service.

Emotions shuddered through Star as, for the first time since she could remember, she felt a sense of optimistic freedom.

Resting

After hours of tireless work, The Engineer returns to a quiet corner of the ship. It powers down momentarily, its lights dimming in a rhythmic pattern, resembling a resting state. The ship, now humming with renewed life.

Elsewhere, gentle snoring came from the men's room as J'Coub slept soundly on the top bunk, one hand still gripping some fabric from his latest project. Alex dreamed a dreamless sleep below him, exhausted physically, but he had drifted off quickly with a sense of achievement.

In the next room, Sorah twisted and turned, her horns occasionally clacking against the bed frame, and Shanice grunted in her sleep each time as she nearly awoke. But the pull of sleep was too strong and she never actually came to full consciousness.

Drifting peacefully in space, Star gently twirled in the air.

All was quiet.

And then the contact alarms rang out across the ship. They were no longer alone.

10. Company

Alex raced to the bridge in just his underwear. The ear-splitting klaxon rang through his head, shaking away the last of his sleep.

"Star! Status report. What is happening?" The ship juddered slightly as Star went into sudden motion and Alex braced himself on the holo-table before easing himself into his seat.

"I believe that the re-activation of my systems has allowed my previous attackers to find us, despite the remoteness of this system." Star explained.

J'Coub, not even bothering with underwear, reached his station and his fingers trembled as they danced across the screen. "I am attempting to hail the Vessel now Captain, do you want to speak to them?"

Alex grimaced a greeting at Shanice and Sorah as they took their stations. Shanice looked absolutely terrified. Sweat glistened on her brow, but Sorah moved with grace and confidence. "Yes, let me know when to speak."

J'Coub met his gaze and nodded.

"This is Captain Alex O'Keefe of the independent vessel Star. The Vrexen that had control of this ship are dead and we are not affiliated with them. I repeat, we are NOT The Vrexen! Please cease fire immediately and talk to us."

He nodded, and J'Coub cut him off. Alex felt an icy calm come over him as he took control of the situation. There was no room for doubt right now."Sorah, Star, what do you make of the enemy vessel?"

Star responded instantly. "Apart from my previous encounter with the vessel, I have no records of a ship of this type in any of my previous encounters or The Vrexen databanks. They are heavily armed and they made no attempt to speak to The Vrexen when they attacked us last time. There were multiple missile impacts before The Vrexen Captain could react. As soon as I sensed them this time, I initiated evasive manoeuvres. It appears I am much more agile than their vessel, and my newfound freedom means my natural reactions are much quicker."

"They are slow but powerful, Captain." Sorah stared at her screen intensely. "It is hard to get accurate readings, but they appear to be armed primarily with a variety of missiles and energy weapons and the hull is heavily armoured. Transferring a visual image of the ship onto the Holo-Table now."

Lights danced across the table in the centre of the room and then an image burst into life. Suspended in mid-air above the table was a huge behemoth of a ship. Alex stared in awe at the looming warship. It was at least twice the size of Star and painted a warlike grey with white symbols daubed across the torpedo-shaped hull.

Rising from the hull almost randomly were dome-shaped weapons attachments and towers that Alex felt looked rather over the top. As he watched, they glinted ominously with light and 3 more missiles streaked towards them. Star narrowly twisted away from them, but the pressure wave from the detonations still shook the ship. "Alex, they are getting closer to hitting me with each volley."

"No response so far, Captain. Want me to try again?" J'Coub asked Alex nervously.

Alex nodded. "One last time then." He stood straighter in his chair and gripped the arm-rests tightly. "Unidentified Vessel. I repeat, we are NOT the Vrexen. We have no quarrel with you and ask that you cease fire immediately or we will be forced to retaliate. This vessel is a living being and its crew are victims of the Vrexen. Please stand down."

For a moment, nothing happened. The enemy ship hung still in space, time slowed as the crew stood tensely waiting for a response, hearts beating fast. Then the comm system crackled to life as the Alien vessel finally responded.

"Abomination. This twisted creature is an ABOMINATION. It and all aboard are tainted and must be eliminated by order of the Divinium Imperium." Came a disgusted sounding growl from the unseen Captain and the com line clicked off sharply. The crew watched in horror as the deadly warship launched a flurry of missiles arching through space to their position.

Stunned for the briefest of moments, Alex looked crestfallen. "Shanice, release the nano-particle cloud. Sorah, return fire. Let's see what some of The Engineers' enhancements can do. J'Coub, once the cloud is released, I want you to run as much interference with it as you can to confuse those missiles." He barked orders in quick succession, his disappointment that his first encounter as captain had turned to violence so quickly replaced with a calm certainty that they could do this.

"We won't let them take us again," he declared with determination.

Shanice activated the Nano-particle cloud and Star turned and spread her tentacles as an immense dark cloud of particles spread out into space. Particles floated free in a fine mist whilst others clumped together, creating a visual and sensor smokescreen around Star.

On the bridge. Sorah leaned back in her chair and pulled controls out from the screen in front of her. The programmable matter forming a visor over her eyes and targeting controls over her hand. "Returning fire Captain. We have nothing that can get through that hull, so targeting enemy weapons systems."

Star shuddered almost imperceptibly as Sorah fired round after round of the massive rail guns at the enemy ship. Super-heated slugs of massively accelerated metal flew towards their target, a few impacting against the hull, but the majority tore through one of the weapon points. The enormous tower listed slightly and then snapped off, drifting away into space, sparking as it did.

"One launcher down, approximately 15 to go. Changing targets now." Sorah immediately adjusted her aim.

"The nano cloud won't last for more than a few minutes, Captain," Shanice said from her station. Alex could hear the tension in her voice as she continued. "They have no visual on us right now and their targeting systems are confused by the reflective particles. What's our plan?"

Alex grimaced again and had to remind himself that despite their newfound knowledge, none of them had faced a situation like this before. "Our weapons themselves are no match for their hull. Escape is an option, but they tracked us once before and we are massively outgunned." He took a breath as his resolve strengthened. "But we can do things that they absolutely can't. Star isn't a ship, she's a living being." He grinned. "Star? How do you feel like a good old wrestling match?"

A ripple ran through the ship. "I have been looking forward to stretching my legs, so to speak, Captain."

Sorah whooped wildly. "Genius! They won't be able to use long-range weapons if we are that close, and I know Star can do a lot of damage that way."

"Foresee any issues, Shanice? J'Coub?" Alex asked. He looked eagerly at his crew.

Shanice looked thoughtful for a moment. "We risk being hit on approach, but that's no different from being hit as we flee. That close? Star could tear that ship apart."

J'Coub didn't look away from his screen as he scanned the information that was displayed there. "I say if we are going to be crazy, let's embrace it!"

Alex sat back in his chair. "Ok Star, once they fire the next volley, let's get in close and fuck them up."

"Inspiring speech Captain. One for the history books." Shanice said wryly.

"Jean-Luc Picard can suck my balls." He joked back to her. "We're a bunch of survivors who have gone through horrific shit to get here. We do things our own way. You ready Star?"

Star's wall glittered with light as she responded. "Brace yourselves team. I'm going to let loose." Soft whirrs and clicks echoed through The Bridge as the automatic safety restraints gently locked into place around each crew member. "There's a lull in firing, I am going...NOW!"

Star shot forward with incredible speed. She emerged from the cloud like a missile, the nano-particles streaming behind, disturbed by her momentum, and the crew pushed back in their seats at the sudden thrust.

Star contracted her body to offer as small a profile as possible, and her long tentacles stretched out behind her. The gap between her and the enemy ship closed quickly as they got a few shots in, glancing off of Star's hull. She felt a rush of adrenaline as some of her old hunting instincts kicked in. Within moments, she was above and past the enemy ship and in an almost impossible change in direction; she darted backwards towards it, her immense tentacles flaring wide to strike. In that moment, Star felt her system flush with a rage she had long since suppressed. Enslaved, tortured, controlled, and now finally free, she was being attacked by people who wanted to exterminate her for the suffering that was forced on her! No more.

On the bridge, Sorah couldn't contain herself and whooped in delight, even as she shook violently around in her restraints. "GO STAR!"

The impact as Star's body wrapped around the dreadnought was surprisingly gentle, but when her tentacles wrapped around the enemy's hull, everyone on board felt it. Star tensed her body as her powerful extremities tightened around the enemy hull, causing a groaning vibration that was heard throughout the ship. She could feel the other ship firing its engines in a desperate attempt to break away, but her grip was too tight and her resolve too strong.

As her tentacles wrap harder around the ship, the thousands of razor sharp suckers, honed to even more deadly sharpness by the artificial adaptations made to her, tore into the outer hull. Originally used for her to grind rocks to feed on the minerals, they now shredded the armour on the Divinium ship without mercy,

The tentacles writhed and twisted, towers and domes ripped and crumbled from the Dreadnought as they tore from the vessel. The ship itself buckled under the immense pressure, the armour plating ripping off in huge chunks. On the Bridge, Alex signalled for J'Coub to hail the enemy ship one more time and wasted no time in addressing them.

"Divinium Imperium. This is your final warning. Stand down completely. Surrender and we will leave you crippled but alive. We did not start this fight, but will not hesitate to finish it."

A momentary pause and then a screeching voice came over the comm system, cries and chaos in the background. "You have DEFILED us. Filth. VERMIN." Alex could almost feel the spittle flying from the alien captain's mouth. "We will be avenged. Your Abomination and all aboard will be scorched from the Universe. Your filthy touch may have prevented my crew from ascending to the Divinium, but the faithful will earn their spears from your deaths. SINNERS. Lower than the…" Alex cut him off abruptly.

"Why won't they talk to us?" Shanice pleaded. "They won't even have a conversation!"

"My Grandfather always used to say that shouting is easier than listening. You can't say I didn't give them a chance." His face was resigned. "Star, let's finish them quickly, with as much mercy as we can."

"Acknowledged Captain." Star's voice held none of Alex's resignation. The rage burning through her was too strong.

Outside, Star contracted one last time. Her powerful tentacles squeezed harder and beneath their relentless assault, the Divinium ship crumpled like a can. Still, she twisted and pulled with all her might until the mighty warship ripped in two and sections of the craft imploded upon exposure to the vacuum of space. With a powerful thrust of her tentacles, she pushed herself away from the fatally wounded ship while explosions ripped through the two halves.

It wasn't the fiery drama that Alex would have imagined before his download, but a series of decompressions through the craft as section after section ruptured and ejected gasses, materials, and bodies into space. As the vessel went dark internally, volatile gasses, fuel, and ammunition reacted to the vacuum of space, creating brief flashes of light.

As Star moved out of reach from the rapidly spreading debris field, the crew on her Bridge didn't hear any noise from the violent destruction, only the soft vibrations through the hull from the carnage outside.

11. Regroup

Almost the entire crew sat quietly in the rec room, while The Engineer, who could not be dissuaded, immediately checked their hull for damage. The air felt heavy in the room as the enormity of what had just happened sank in to the crew.

Shanice sat curled up in her chair, feet on the seat and knees tucked in under her chin. Her eyes fixed on the table ahead and she was perfectly still. J'Coub had left The Bridge immediately to return to his quarters to get dressed and now sat forward in his chair, both hands on the table and his back straight, rather than his usual slouch. He had thoughtfully brought hot drinks for everyone.

Sorah clutched her hot drink in both hands and sat alert and attentive, sipping it carefully.

Alex also took a moment to change and wore his old grey sweatpants and white T-shirt that he had been abducted in, but now clean and fresh. He gave the crew a moment more before he spoke. "I know this was a massively stressful event and a huge thing to process. Before we get to any of that, though, I just wanted to say that I am SO proud of you all and how you handled yourselves here. We got out of this alive because of each of your actions. Star, I am talking to you here as well." He stood behind his chair, too wired to sit down. Leaning forward and putting his weight on his hands. "That was an awful decision made back there. The right decision, I am sure, but awful anyway." He paused for breath and looked up at the team one by one. "We were cornered into an almost impossible situation against an enemy that was, by all appearances, determined to wipe us out regardless of what we could have said to them." He turned to Shanice. "I can see that you are struggling the most with this Shan. How are you feeling?"

Shanice hugged her knees tighter. "I don't know, to be honest, Alex. I understand the stakes. The way they reacted to us. I know they attacked first. But I just can't get my head around how many people could have been on that ship. Did they all think like that? Were there cooks or janitors or passengers on board? I mean, I worked in a fucking call centre for an energy firm back home. Lots of people hated the company and what they did, but it was just a job for me. Was there a Shanice over there answering the comms to pay her version of student loans?"

Shanice's words hung heavy in the air, her inner turmoil reflecting the complexity of their situation. The crew remained silent, each lost in their own thoughts, grappling with the magnitude of what had transpired.

Alex nodded slowly, his face a mixture of understanding and empathy. "Those are tough questions, Shanice, and honestly, I don't have all the answers. What we faced out there was not just a ship; it seemed like an ideology, a belief system that saw us as nothing more than abominations. We defended ourselves, but the cost..." He trailed off, his gaze drifting towards the void outside the window.

J'Coub interjected softly, "In the Gallery, I saw many perspectives. Artists often question the value of life and the weight of actions, and a single piece could mean a hundred things to different people. But this, this is different. It's real, not conceptual. I think we're all feeling that weight now."

Sorah set her cup down, her voice steady but sombre. "In my training, it showed me that to defend ourselves, to protect our community, is the most important thing. But this... this was on a scale I never imagined. I feel a sense of duty fulfilled, but also a heaviness. It's a hard reconciliation, but I think we did the right thing. I will sleep tonight knowing that, but my dreams may not be pleasant."

Alex looked around the room, his eyes lingering on each crew member, acknowledging their shared experience. "We're in this together, every step of the way. It's okay to feel these emotions, to question our actions. That's part of our strength. That is the reason we have survived what we have been through. We empathise, we feel, and we grow from these experiences."

He took a deep breath before continuing, "What we did today was about survival, about protecting not just ourselves, but a being that has become dear to us all. Star, you're more than just a ship to us."

Star's voice, warm yet tinged with sadness, filled the room. "Thank you, Alex, and everyone. I never desired violence, but the actions we took were necessary for our survival. I mourn the loss of life, but I also cherish the lives saved here today. Your lives."

The room fell into a reflective silence, each crew member processing the events and their feelings. The weight of their choices was palpable. But today, the bond between them had faced a test and grown stronger because of it. They were no longer just a crew; they were becoming a family, united in their journey and the trials they had faced together.

Shanice reached forwards and took her warm mug from the table in front of her. "I know. I don't see any other way we could have dealt with this. But I think, if this ever becomes something I don't feel the weight of, then it's time to put me back into stasis."

J'Coub reached across and put a hand on Shanice's forearm. "I know how traumatising that must have been for you, but I promise the next time I will wear trousers."

Shanice didn't quite laugh, but she felt the tension lift slightly from her shoulders. "At least I know you will be ok if you are cracking those awful jokes."

Sorah lifted her mug in the air slightly. "To be honest, from what I now know, I think this is maybe the first ever space battle where The Captain was in his underpants!" The three of them turned to look at Alex.

He finally took a seat at the table with the rest of them. "I was just thankful we didn't have visual communication with them. If this was a religious race like it seemed, can you imagine how much more offended they may have been?" He smiled sadly and took a swig from his drink. "Ok, Team, there are a few things we need to discuss. First is, what do we do now? We have already made enemies of two races, The Vrexen and the Divinium, simply for existing. We can't stay here, obviously, as I am sure that wreckage will be investigated soon. Opening the floor to you all for thoughts, feeling and ideas."

Sorah spoke immediately. "First, we need to retreat to somewhere safe. It feels like all the work we have done to repair Star is just the start. Second, we need to find out more about The Divinium and The Vrexen and work out how to avoid them or defend ourselves from them better. Third, we need to find better weapons. The stronger we are, the less likely someone will attack us. The trick we used was fine against one vessel, but useless against more."

J'Coub tapped the table as he spoke. "Yes! We need more information. The download was amazing, but they didn't use any Vrexen brains in Omni, so weirdly we are lacking information, even about them. I think we also need somewhere quiet to really get used to what Star can do. I wouldn't even have thought about that grab we did. I have only ever seen long distance space battles."

Star gently spoke. "I agree. It is so long since I was free to act as I pleased. Instinct alone drove me today, and rage, but that will not be enough in the future."

Alex nodded. "Thank you Star, I agree. Shanice?"

Shanice looked down at the table and her face flushed slightly. "There's something we haven't discussed yet. I feel bad even bringing it up. But what is the possibility of going home?" She grew quiet momentarily, but quickly interjected. "Once Star is safe, I mean. Do any of us want to?"

"I cannot ask more of you than you have already done." Star said earnestly. "I will take anyone home that wants too, but there is something to consider first. Something I am ashamed to say I have not yet mentioned."

The team looked shocked and thoughtful about Shanice's statement and Star's response.

"I am staying!" Sorah exclaimed suddenly. "With what I know now, there's no way I can go back. If you will have me, Star, that is."

"What haven't you mentioned, Star?" Alex asked.

"You all have a home here with me if you so choose." Star said. "But I feel you should know that your time in stasis was quite significant. Alex and Shanice, by time standards on your home planet. You were both taken around 19 years ago. J'Coub around 15 and Sorah 5."

Shanice looked stunned. "19 years?" Her feet hit the floor as they slipped under the table.

"Holy shit." Alex looked almost as shocked as Shanice, his face paling as he took the information in. "That's a long time."

J'Coub's eyes narrowed slightly. "It doesn't really change anything for me. The gallery wasn't doing that well, so I imagine it has already changed hands. My partners and I weren't very serious and, as I said before, I'm not exactly close to my family." He paused briefly. "To be honest, this is the first time in my life I have ever really felt useful. Like I have some kind of direction."

"My family!" Shanice reeled again, tears welling in the corners of her eyes. "They must think I'm long dead. 19 years, Lord Jesus, my nieces will be older than me now!"

The room fell silent as they all processed this new information, broken only by a soft beep from the corridor as The Engineer appeared at the entrance. He looked around the room and the expressions of the people sat around the table. Almost without hesitation, he dashed to Shanice's side and gently scanned her face, paying particular attention to the tears running freely down her cheek. He whined sadly, and a port opened on his side. A manipulator arm appeared with a soft cloth on the end and the enigmatic robot gently held it out for Shanice.

This unexpected action just caused Shanice to cry harder as she mumbled thanks to him through gasping breaths. He floated there a moment longer before spinning around and flying quickly off the bridge.

Sorah moved her chair next to Shanice and put her arm around her. "I can't believe a nano-tech based AI, just put us all to shame with its show of empathy." She pulled Shanice in close. "It's ok. Whatever you decide, we are with you all the way. You helped me so much when I first awoke and in all of our late night talks. Let me help you now. Do you need anything?"

Shanice hugged Sorah close, the soft feel of the aliens fur both grounded her and comforted her. "I just need some time to process this. That's all. Maybe if J'Coub has worked out how to make wine by now, we could all commiserate or celebrate together later once we are safe?"

J'Coub placed a hand gently on her back. "I am sure I can rustle something up. Alex? How do you feel? Do you have family back home too?"

Alex turned to look at J'Coub and gently shook his head."It was just me and my grandfather. He was close to dying from Alzheimers, so he won't be there anymore. I have been thinking about that a lot anyway, as he only had so little time left. My life was just looking after him and working to get by. I don't think I had even re-started my life properly after the accident." He rubbed his arm idly, as if comforting himself. "I'm with you J'Coub, truth be told, I haven't felt so alive in years."

J'Coub smiled at him, genuine warmth and sympathy apparent on his face. "I guess there's no reason we can't go visit our homes from time to time once this is all over? Theres definitely a lot of things I would love to pick up and bring with us. Shanice would definitely stay if I brought a bottle of Gravillian Blue on board, I am sure." He ruffled her hair affectionately.

Shanice smiled weakly and knocked his hand away. "IF I stay, the first rule is you never touch a Black Woman's hair. Ok?"

"Erogenous zone?" He asked jokingly?

"Half a cultural thing and half the fact that these extensions were expensive." She teased back.

At this, the tension in the air lifted slightly. Alex looked at his team proudly. "Take as long as you need to decide, Shanice. For now, Star, do you know of anywhere we can go that will be safe for now?"

"I have several options in mind, Captain," Star said. "I have been thinking of where to go since I arrived here. Would you like to hear my top 3 choices?"

"Please go ahead."

"Option 1 is an old research facility I once passed on my travels. It is in a nebula that interferes with scanners. It will not only be difficult to find, but may contain valuable materials we can use."

"Option 2. I am aware of a rogue planet drifting through space, untethered to a solar system. There are old lava tunnels large enough for us to hide in. There are few natural resources on this planet, however, this means that we are less likely to encounter visitors."

"Option 3 is an abandoned mega-structure that my people once used as navigation point. We have never been inside, but there are no signs of life. There is the possibility that there may be advanced technology inside we could use, but I do not know how safe this option would be."

"What is a mega-structure?" Shanice asked, her curiosity peaked.

Star responded almost immediately. "It is a vast structure in space. This one completely encloses its system's sun, capturing and utilising all the energy it produces."

A loud and insistent beeping chimed through the comms system and everyone jumped in shock.

Star interjected. "Do not panic. I am afraid that The Engineer is patched into our comms and has become rather enthused at the idea of exploring the mega-structure. He appears to be adamantly pleading his case."

"I nearly needed to change my clothes again!" Alex sighed in relief. "Well, I have to say if we have to hide somewhere, then that sounds like the coolest one."

Sorah's ears flicked back and forth. "I too would like to see this Sun Sphere."

"A space station large enough to surround a sun? Imagine what could be inside?" J'Coub gushed. "Who built it? Why was it abandoned? I totally vote yes!" He almost bounced in his seat.

Shanice looked up and around the table. "I suppose if we are going to do this weird sci-fi shit, we might as well pick the weirdest ways to do it. As long as it doesn't turn out to be a Death Star, because not gonna lie, it SOUNDS like a Death Star."

Alex chuckled. "Well, that's an easy vote. Tell The Engineer he wins easily. Where is he, anyway?"

Star's voice went quiet. "He left the ship rather quickly after hearing what Shanice said. I believe he is on the destroyed enemy ship, collecting the dead and ensuring that they are stored together in a relatively undamaged section so that their families can find them."

The room fell into quiet contemplation once more as they weighed up the ramifications of the gentle robot's actions and the depth of his ability to understand emotion.

The team sat around the central table on The Bridge looking at a representation of Star from the outside. The Engineer had returned from its solemn duties and had let Star know he had taken detailed scans of the Alien craft and some downloaded data from their main computers for the team to look at later to see if they could work out more about the unknown enemy. He now hovered next to the table and beeped excitedly at what they were about to experience.

"I think it is easier if I just show you." Star said, her lights glittering with excitement. "The way I traverse space quickly is a little different. It takes a huge amount of energy to do it, so I need a significant amount of time between jumps, but I can take us to the mega-structure almost instantaneously. Are you ready?"

Alex stared at the image intensely. "Let's do it! The sooner we are out of here, the better."

"Yes Captain. Initiating jump now." Star said.

All four of the crew members leaned forward almost imperceptibly at the same time. The Engineer span its body around, arms tightened against him. On the screen, the image of star seemed to shorten slightly, and the crew felt a shudder run through them as Star gently extended her tentacles from trailing behind her, up along the length of her body until they met, tip to tip, just in front of the bow.

Blue and white light pulsed down each tentacle faster and faster until the tips of each one began to crackle and glow with energy. The energy grew brighter until a large area glowed in front of them. Just as the light grew almost too bright to look at, Star pulled her tentacles apart, showing a small tear in space and a different star scape on the other side.

"Incredible!" Alex's eyes were wide as he watched the jaw dropping display on the table in front of him.

There were gasps and exclamations from all around the table as Star literally pulled the tear wider and wider until it was large enough for her to move her body through. Metre by metre, she gracefully slipped through the tear, her tentacles gripping the edge and pushing her through into the unknown. As Star cleared the tear, they watched as her tentacles behind her once again danced with the same light, neatly closing the tear until it was dark once again. Star then pulled her tentacles back and coiled them once more.

"We have arrived at the outskirts of our destination system." Star's voice almost purred with pleasure. "It is easier and safer for me to jump to the outer edge of a solar system that I rarely visit. We will arrive at the mega-structure in approximately 2 ship days."

The Engineer whined in disappointment before Star replied. "Yes, I know you want to be there now. You know as well as I do we risk an accident if I jumped further in."

He waved his manipulator arms around wildly as he emitted a high-pitched whirr.

"Well, I am organic, mostly, so that is closer to an insult than you realise."

The Engineer made a sad BOOP noise and drew his arms in, compacting his size. With a final, almost obscene sounding noise, he floated off The Bridge.

"My apologies crew, although I understand his eagerness, there was no need for that behaviour. I am sure he will apologise soon."

Shanice actually laughed out loud, then raised her hand to her mouth as if she hadn't expected it. "It's fine. You should hear the language Sorah uses in the morning!"

Sorah elbowed her gently. "Maybe I would be in a better mood if you didn't talk so much in your sleep. Honestly, if you were one of my tribe, you would have been the first one eaten in a raid. You make so much noise!"

J'Coub stood and spread his hands. "On that note, I have things to do before Alex starts talking about my snoring." He did a mock bow and left the bridge.

Alex nodded. "I need to go through that data to see what I can learn about the Divinium. I won't be able to rest until I know a bit more. Besides, I need to distract myself with something or I am going to get as excited as The Engineer. I'll catch you guys later."

He stood and walked off The Bridge towards the Rec Room. Sorah turned to Shanice. "Are you doing ok? Want to hang out some more?"

Shanice smiled at her friend. "Thanks, that would be lovely, but I have a lot to think about. I'm going to head off for a nana nap. Catch up with you later though? Girl's night in?"

"What is a nana nap? Sorry, that didn't translate fully for me."

"Hah, sorry. Older people on my planet tend to fall asleep a lot in the afternoon. A Nana is slang for Grandmother." She winked at her friend. "Not that I need age as an excuse. I LOVE a nap."

Sorah gently raised herself up from the table. "Then nap soundly, friend. Girl's night sounds amazing."

12. Buddy

"What do you think this is about?" Shanice asked as she walked alongside Alex and Sorah through Star's corridors, following the glittering trail of light bugs that led to their mysterious destination.

Alex shrugged his shoulders. "No idea. Star? Any clues?"

"I am afraid I am sworn to secrecy, Captain. J'Coub threatened to paint me pink if I told you. Besides, I really don't want to ruin the surprise." The ship replied.

Sorah's face crinkled in amusement as she imagined the powerful living ship painted a lurid pink. "I'm thinking he's discovered more of those crab things, or something exciting in deep storage."

"He reminds me of some actors I have known in the past, so I'm putting my money on a one-man play. 4 hours long and detailing all his past romantic conquests." Shanice joked. "Alex? What's your best guess?"

The Captain looked pensive for a moment. "Probably more food for us to taste. Which I'm okay with, as the last few have been pretty good to be fair."

"Well, anything to distract us is good. We are still a day and a half away from the mega-structure. Or 27.75 Ships hours."

Shanice remarked. "I'm rarely that precise, but The Engineer keeps zooming up to me to display a countdown, spinning madly and dashing off again."

"Me too."/"Same here." came Alex and Sorah's voices at the same time.

"The little guy's more excited than a kid at Christmas." Alex continued. "It makes sense considering his race."

Sorah looked at Alex. "I'm embarrassed that I haven't really asked more about him. What are his people like?"

"Well, according to Star, He is from a race that calls themselves 'The Builders'. Descended from AI driven utility robots and construction assistants. After their biological creators went extinct from a combination of warfare and disease, they slowly evolved into a fully autonomous species. Did I get that right Star?" He asked.

"Indeed, Alex. His people are on the whole a peaceful and insular race. The vast majority stay on their homeworld. Their original function has become somewhat of a driving impulse for them, even though they are not bound by programming any more." Star explained. "Oh, you should see his world! Constantly changing and evolving as buildings are improved, torn down and rebuilt. Each version is more beautiful than the last. Their bodies, too, change on a whim as they remake themselves in the latest fashion or style, or upgraded for whatever function they choose in that moment."

Sorah "That sounds incredible. No wonder he has been spending a lot of time with J'Coub recently. Two art lovers together."

The trail of light bugs appeared to end at an unfamiliar door, the little creatures forming a frame around the entrance.

"Here we are! Who wants to go in first?" Shanice asked warily. "Where are we anyway?"

Alex nodded to himself, subconsciously tucking his t-shirt in as he realised where they were from the knowledge in his download. "Formal dining room, part of the VIP suite. Looks like I was right."

Alex didn't hesitate to go through the door first. As the bio-skin pulled back and allowed him entry, music drifted towards them from the room beyond."

Inside was a stunningly beautiful room. Bone spurs arched towards the ceiling, where they met in an intricate pattern. Organic, flowing shelves lined the walls, seemingly growing directly from the structure of Star herself. Glowing bioluminescent plants in a myriad of colours cast a gentle ambient light throughout the room. A soft, moss-like carpet covered the floor, giving the impression of walking on a forest floor.

In the centre of the room stood a large, oval table, crafted from a smooth, dark material that reflected the ambient light like a tranquil pool under moonlight. Around the table stood elegantly designed chairs, each one slightly different from the other, yet all harmoniously blending into the room's organic aesthetics.

Towards one wall some shimmering cloth draped a large object and beside it, another wall of the room was completely transparent, offering a breathtaking view of the star-studded void outside. The stars seemed so close; it felt to Alex as though he could reach out and touch them.

Above the table, a delicate chandelier, resembling a cluster of luminescent jellyfish, hung from the ceiling. Its soft, pulsating glow provided a gentle illumination, enhancing the magical ambiance of the room.

J'Coub stood proudly at the far end of the room, clearly pleased with himself. An assortment of exotic-looking dishes and drinks adorned the table, with each emitting a tantalising aroma. Some Alex recognised from previous successful taste tests, but others were new.

As the rest of the crew entered, their expressions transformed from curiosity to awe. The Engineer hovered next to J'Coub, a tray of glasses delicately balanced on one of his manipulator arms.

"Welcome friends." J'Coub bowed dramatically. "I felt that after what we have been through, we all deserved a little downtime while we wait to reach our destination."

The glasses on The Engineers plate wobbled slightly as the machine couldn't stop himself from displaying a countdown on the wall that said '27.25 Ship Hours'

J'Coub gave the little robot a sideward glance and cleared his throat. "There is good food, good company and, most importantly, a passable attempt at wine. Sit and enjoy!" He gestured towards the seats.

As the crew took their seats, they each expressed admiration for what J'Coub had created for them. "This looks incredible J, you have been holding out on us!" Shanice's face looked delighted as she took in the spread before them.

"I agree." Sorah added, smiling up at their friend. "This is very thoughtful of you, J'Coub."

Alex took his seat, amazed at how comfortable it felt, even compared to the Captain's chair. "I think this is very much needed. I am adding Welfare Officer to your ever-growing list of titles. Thank you, friend."

J'Coub grinned and gestured towards The Engineer who circled the table, deftly placing a glass of sparkling amber liquid next to each of the crew.

"Thanks, buddy." Shanice said as she sniffed the liquid inside.

The Engineer paused in midair and pointed an arm towards his core, emitting an excited squeal.

"What's up?" Shanice asked. "Have I said something wrong?"

Star's voice, relaying through the comm system, responded. "He really enjoyed being called buddy."

Alex raised his glass and tapped lightly with a fork to get everyone's attention. "Ok, then that's our first toast. For the crew on board, the six of us, our friend here is henceforth to be called Buddy." He raised his glass and took a swig.

The crew followed suit and Buddy, as he was now known, burbled excitedly.

Shanice gripped her glass and stared intently at the liquid inside. "J'Coub, this is fantastic. And I am not just saying that because it's the first taste of alcohol I have had in 19 years!"

J'Coub waved his hand dismissively. "Pfft. It is adequate at best. Just you wait until I have some proper supplies. We brewed a selection of our own liqueurs for the gallery bar back home. Some even won awards."

Sorah took another sip of the mildly sweet, effervescent liquid. The tastes reminding her vaguely of the sweet cakes her tribe made to celebrate the harvest. "May we perhaps have a bottle of this? Shanice and I are planning a girl's night."

J'Coub nodded in assent, clearly thrilled with their reactions. "I have made 10 bottles so far, so feel free. But we should try to make them last for now."

Shanice grinned wildly. "In anticipation of this momentous occasion, I have also whipped up something in Med bay that will sober us up quickly AND prevent hangovers, so it won't affect our duties."

Alex raised his glass again. "Last time I got drunk was in my local. Grotty place called The Coven near Yarm where I lived, but we called it 'The Claggy Mat'. Nice change drinking in here as my feet don't stick to the floor!"

There was a whistle from the end of the table as their host nodded appreciatively at her. "Please, eat!" He declared, and then reached under the table and pulled out a bowl of soft glowing orbs. "And these, Buddy, are for you. Micro power cells in a powdered coating of rare metals. I hope you like it."

Buddy made a modulated wooOOoo sound and moved one of his manipulator arms forward. The spheres varied in size and colour, looking to Alex like bizarre, glowing chocolate truffles. A stream of nanites coated one particular blue sphere, dusted in silver powder and artfully decorated with tiny rocks and crystals, and slowly broke it down into atoms as the energy flowed up his arm into his core. After a brief pause, he beeped in appreciation and practically snatched the bowl out of J'Coub's hands, hovering in his space around the table to continue eating.

The room buzzed with conversation as they all relaxed into the meal. The various dishes were all roundly appreciated as the variety of flavours and textures made a welcome change from the staple green mush that had been the backbone of their meals here so far. Alex tucked into an aromatic bowl of what looked like spaghetti, but tasted of a savoury stew. The meaty scent made his mouth water with each bite.

Sorah was delighted to enjoy a bowl of leafy greens and delicate scented flowers that J'Coub had carefully sourced from some plants around the ship. Being a herbivore, she missed the sweet and peppery flavours and the crunch of the salad that she now had.

On the opposite side of the table, Shanice had a variety of food on her plate, but seemed most enamoured by a red, eye watering powder that the silver alien had provided as a condiment, liberally sprinkling it over her meal.

As the evening progressed, the crew laughed and sympathised. They shared stories of their home planets and quietly talked about the earlier attack. Once the second bottle was done and a third opened, J'Coub stood up to get everyone's attention.

"I have one more surprise for you all before we retire." He gestured towards the object to his left that was still covered by its shroud. Realising this was his cue, Buddy flew towards the object and gripped a corner of the cloth. "Buddy and I have been working on this on and off for a while now, and I think we are now ready to share. Buddy, if you will?"

The little Builder paused for dramatic effect and then beeped out a fanfare as he pulled the cover away. Underneath, four uniforms hung neatly from a rack. Alex, Shanice and Sorah all broke out into polite applause, sensing the effort the two others had put into this dramatic reveal.

J'Coub walked over to the rack and admired his handiwork for a moment. "I based these on the protective suits we found in engineering and modified them further with Buddy and the maintenance crabs. Self adjusting for fit, responsive to their environment and uniquely adaptive to the wearer's needs. We enhanced their original purpose to create something comfortable and durable, suited for everyday wear."

"Wow, they look amazing." Shanice exclaimed. "I can confirm the original version was really comfy."

"Indeed. Buddy kindly donated some of his limited supply of nanobots, and the crabs have helped weave a bio layer within each suit. This means the suits are self cleaning, self healing and monitor and adapt to both your needs and external factors. If you need to go into a non-breathable atmosphere, the helmet can auto engage and the bio layer will absorb the carbon dioxide you exhale and transform it back into oxygen at an accelerated rate. A nano-skin layer based on Star's hull will harden upon impact to prevent injury, effectively turning the outfit into armour as and when needed."

He pulled each uniform out one by one as he went. "Each suit also has a small but powerful exoskeleton woven into it to enhance performance. Sorah, you will be excited to hear that this not only enhances your strength and speed, but with the helmet engaged either fully or partially, it will also enhance your eyesight and hearing." He paused briefly. "In addition to the armoured coating, we also took inspiration from her camouflage ability, allowing the suit to blend into your surroundings, or, if you so choose, to alter its appearance to a limited degree."

He walked around the table and handed a suit out to each member of the team. "These can be worn around the clock comfortably and cleanly, so we need never risk a repeat of having to deal with an enemy attack in the nude."

Alex took his suit almost reverently. "I'm speechless. Guys, this is amazing. I can't believe what you have achieved here, its nothing short of…"

"I'm trying mine on!" Shanice screamed as she ran into the stateroom adjoining the Dining room.

"Me too!" Sorah practically leapt from her chair and followed her.

"I am sure that would have been a very inspiring speech, Captain." J'Coub said wryly. "But shall we get dressed for dessert?" He gestured to one of the other staterooms, and Alex needed no more encouragement. He pushed his chair back and went to leave the room.

"Thank you J'Coub. I really mean it." He said in the doorway.

"Oh, nonsense." J'Coub said. "It took less effort to make than it did not commenting on your awful taste in clothes. Now go!"

Alex gripped the outfit closer, paused for a moment, then walked into the stateroom, closing the door behind him. He barely took a moment to look at the luxurious surroundings, instead quickly slipping off his clothes and easing into the sleek grey jumpsuit. The fabric was buttery soft as it slid over his hips; he felt no trace of the metal or bone integrated into the uniform. Easing one arm into a sleeve and then the other, he marvelled as the suit gently adjusted to his frame, softly gripping his body.

Next came a flush of warmth as it adjusted the internal temperature to suit Alex's needs. The whole thing fit like a glove, even the foot coverings gently solidified over the sole of his feet to provide a soft but firm base to walk on. Thin lines snaked down from the wrists onto his hands and down his fingers, then gently expanded into gloves. Alex ran his hands over the suit and was amazed to realise that he felt everything as if he was bare handed, the suit providing haptic feedback through the fabric.

Reaching up to the collar like Shanice had told him, he pressed the button on his neck. The bone claws stretched up from his nape and gently gripped his head as the transparent helmet enveloped his face. Suddenly, lights blinked on as a HUD appeared in front of him and information flickered across his view. Details on the space, temperature, status of the ship and whereabouts of the crew were dotted the screen.

With another tap of the button, the helmet reduced to a visor across his eyes, the information still visible but automatically shifting to a more compact view. Satisfied, Alex promised himself that they would all have time to explore the suit's full capabilities soon, and he turned back and returned to the main room.

Alex was the last of the team to re-emerge. Sorah, Shanice and J'Coub stood by the giant window excitedly comparing suits. He took a moment to appreciate how striking they all looked against the backdrop of space. "Well, don't you guys look the part!" He remarked as he joined the trio.

Shanice's suit was a deep forest green with gold piping down the seams, J'Coub had altered his to a blue and silver combination that echoed his natural tones and Sorah had deepened the grey of her uniform to a smart black which stood out against her white fur. "Oh, you all changed the colours already!"

Shanice looked him up and down. "I'm so used to seeing you in grey and white that I think you could just adjust it to those colours to be honest. Smart but utilitarian. Here let me." She walked over to him and tapped away on the small screen on the back of his glove and the suit altered its colours to a light grey. The sleeves turned white, bleeding up onto his shoulders and white piping mirrored that on Shanice and J'Coub. "There, what do you think?"

Alex took a moment to look at himself in the window's reflection and nodded appreciatively. "I like it! I think we all look fantastic."

Shanice smiled and wiped some imaginary dirt from his shoulder. "We do indeed. Looking at us now, I can't believe how far we have come! We look like we belong now."

"We do belong." Sorah interjected. "I just wanted to say, Star, Buddy, everyone here… You have helped me become something far more than I ever dreamed of being. No matter what happens in the future, or what we each decide to do. You will always be my tribe."

"Aw, Sorah!" Shanice went over and hugged her friend. "I feel the same, and I promise that isn't just the wine talking."

J'Coub beamed proudly and patted Buddy affectionately on his chassis. "I suppose you are all more tolerable than most people I deal with."

"I'm so proud of us all." Alex said, before holding up a hand defensively. "No speeches, I promise. I know you all just interrupt me. But, just, thank you is all. Thank you." He went to raise a toast but squinted in surprise as a bright light shone in his eyes. '23.75 Ship Hours' appeared projected on Alex's face as his visor deployed automatically. Buddy chortled electronically.

Alex sighed in defeat. "On that note, I think I am going to call it a night before I set Buddy to cleaning the waste filters. Tomorrow, let's put these suits through their paces in the morning, get a real feel for what they can do. Then we can get ready to explore the mega structure early evening."

13. Ship Hours

The crew arose later than usual and met for a leisurely breakfast before heading to the training room.

"I didn't even know we had a training room and I'm supposed to be the information officer." J'Coub whined.

"It was originally one of the Hanger Bays," Sorah explained. "After the initial attack, there was an enormous hole in the hull and the shuttles here were vented into space. I figured we have another Hanger Bay anyway and because this one is a fairly isolated from the main operational areas, nobody would miss it."

"Buddy and I cleared the space after he had patched the hole in the hull, then when I learned of the maintenance crabs, we reinforced the space and turned some of the junk into training equipment. Shanice and I have been coming in here most mornings to train."

Shanice shrugged her shoulders. "She drags me here every morning is what she means."

Sorah ignored her and carried on their tour. "SO, we have weights made from compacted ship materials, a climbing wall we assembled from salvaged panels, Shanice painted out a running track around the space and then Buddy added various controls that let us play with things like gravity, air and temperature. We want to add an obstacle course next."

Shanice pointed to a circle in the centre of the space. "Over there is the sparring ring where Sorah kicks my arse. The other corner is where I cry and finally, just by the door, I had the crabs install one of the healing pods in case anyone gets injured."

Sorah clapped her on her shoulder. "She's being modest. Shanice is very agile and has been teaching me something called Zumba, which is a very complicated dance. Yoga, which seems to be a stretching exercise before a fight and her aim with a pistol, is well above average."

"House of the Dead in the local arcades. Classic wasted youth." Shanice shrugged.

J'Coub chuckled, glancing around the enormous room with a newfound appreciation. "Well, it seems I've been missing out on quite the adventure in here!"

Alex, adjusting the sleeves of his suit, nodded in agreement. "Great work, all of you, crabs included!"

"I'm itching to try the climbing wall in this outfit." Sorah spoke up as she moved to the wall area whilst engaging her visor. Without hesitation, she leapt onto the wall effortlessly, catching the first hand grip she saw. "Incredible. Not only does the HUD show you your best route, but it enhances my agility and strength." She quickly climbed to the top of the wall, her movements fluid and precise. Upon reaching the top, she let her body hang from the wall, with only one hand holding her in her place. "Yep, this is amazing! No excuse for not training naturally, but we should definitely use these in addition." With one push, she bounced off the wall and landed gracefully at the base.

Shanice, meanwhile, had taken off around the running track. The only thing in the room she was fully comfortable with exercise wise. Her medical mind began subconsciously testing the suit's response to rapid movement and direction changes. Lap after lap, she ran as the others worked and played around her. She was amazed by how the suit adjusted to her movements, offering support and flexibility without restricting her speed.

As she ran, she forgot all about the others in the room or her lingering doubts from the attack and just fell into the moment, the only sensations she was focusing on were her steady breathing, the rhythmic impact of her feet on the ground and the feel of the air against her face.

J'Coub, ever the curious one, was fascinated by the environmental controls. He experimented with the gravity settings in one corner of the space, first reducing it to experience a moon-like bounce, then increasing it to feel the strain on his muscles. He laughed with delight, clearly enjoying the new sensations, especially as one of the maintenance crabs somehow managed to waddle into the gravity field and soon drifted confused past J'Coub's head..

Alex gave the sparring ring a try, motioning for Sorah to join him after her climb. As they engaged in a friendly sparring match, Alex found the suit's responsive armour engaging at the right moments, cushioning the impact of Sorah's well-placed strikes.

"The feedback on these suits is amazing," Alex commented between breaths. "It's like they're a part of us."

"I'm impressed with your hand to hand skills, Captain. Your time as a warrior shows." Sorah countered, as she missed another hit.

Buddy, who had been quietly observing from the sidelines, suddenly zipped into the centre of the ring, projecting a holographic display of different combat moves and styles. It seemed he was eager to contribute to the training session in his own unique way, but the distraction caused Alex to falter, allowing Sorah to sweep his legs from under him, and he hit the mat with a crash.

As the morning progressed, laughter and playful banter filled the training room, creating a lively atmosphere. The crew took turns trying out different exercises, pushing the limits of their new suits, and discovering their enhanced capabilities. Shanice even managed to coax J'Coub into trying Zumba, leading to a hilarious and slightly uncoordinated dance session that had everyone in stitches.

"Never thought I'd see the day where J'Coub dances," Alex chuckled, watching as J'Coub awkwardly moved to the rhythm, his suit subtly assisting his movements to keep him from falling over.

"Neither did I, Captain, at least not sober," J'Coub replied, slightly out of breath but grinning. "But I have to admit, this is quite fun. And these suits... they're incredible, even if I do say so myself."

As they wrapped up their training session, Sorah gathered everyone in the centre of the room. "I think we should make this a regular thing. Not just for physical training, but to strengthen our bond as a tribe. We've come through a lot together, and this," she gestured around the room, "this is a symbol of our resilience and unity."

The crew nodded in agreement, feeling energised by their experience. They headed back to the Rec Room for lunch. As they walked, their suits silently adjusted back to their regular mode, disposing of any sweat and grime and compensating for any bruises landed.

12.03 Ship Hours

Over lunch in the Rec Room, the atmosphere was light and filled with animated conversation. Shanice playfully recounted J'Coub's dance moves, eliciting laughter from the group. "Honestly, J, you've got some moves hidden in there!" she teased.

J'Coub retorted with a smile, "Well, maybe I'll surprise you all with a full dance routine one day. You never know."

Alex pointed his fork at Shanice and a blob of food fell off. "You needn't talk. You were running for nearly an entire hour with this weird smile on your face. None of us wanted to disturb you. Buddy was even tailing you for about 7 laps before he got bored and went off to play with the weights."

Shanice sat back in her chair, her bowl already empty. "I always loved to run. I'd run through Peckham Rye Park every morning before work. There's something about it that is so freeing. Besides, if you want to get into acting, you need to look a certain way."

"I think that was the first time I really let loose since my back healed. Honestly, can't tell you how good that felt." Alex speared the fallen food and popped it into his mouth. The smokey meat taste was reminiscent of turkey bacon and his mouth watered. He took a few pieces in his hand and surreptitiously dropped them under the table where the maintenance crabs were waiting eagerly. Having also been test subjects for J'Coub's culinary experiment, they were now a little obsessed with the meals he had created. "If only we had a swimming pool on board, oh and maybe a jacuzzi."

"You could always go for a dip in the brain tank." Shanice shuddered slightly at the recollection. "Not what I'd call relaxing, mind you."

Alex looked down at the pinkish lumps of food in front of him and gently pushed the bowl away. "Yeah. I'll pass."

9.26 Ship Hours

"What do you mean, the pads fold down?" Sorah asked, holding hers in front of her as if it was something she had never seen before.

"Well, yeah. It's a flexible screen. You can roll it up, fold it smaller or there's an option for a holo-display as well. Have you been carrying yours around full sized?"

Sorah stuttered for a moment. "YES! It's so annoying. I keep putting it down to do things and walking away without it."

Shanice laughed gently. "I'm sorry. I sometimes think these downloads gave us everything, but there are still a lot of gaps, I guess." She took Sorah's pad from her hands and showed the fold for her. "See, and if you fold it to this size, it mounts directly on the wrist of your suit. It's always communicating with your visor, but attaching it gives it a slight boost."

Sorah took the folded pad and experimentally attached it to her wrist. "Hmph." She exclaimed and then walked out of their shared room.

8.01 Ship Hours

Alex entered the remaining shuttle bay, curious about what lay inside from Sorah's earlier description. He couldn't believe that they had not yet explored this area. The room mirrored the one that the team had converted into a training area, but had a sleek utilitarian look. There was little trace of Star's organic elements in this space, instead thick blast panels lined the walls and harsh artificial light illuminated the space.

The space had small craft arrayed around it, almost like a museum or showroom, with neat rows along the floor and others displayed hanging from rails along the ceiling. Every single ship looked distinct from the others in design and size and it dawned on Alex that they were a solid testament to the abductions The Vrexen had perpetrated against various races throughout the years.

One ship close to him looked sleek and aerodynamic, with vast engines on either side and only a single cockpit. Its glossy red exterior reminded him of a sports car. This ship looked designed to race.

Next to it, in stark contrast, was an ugly utilitarian shuttle. Manipulator arms jutted out in front of it and its faded yellow hull was dull and workmanlike. Obviously used to manoeuvre cargo or assist in construction, it sat there bulky and rusting.

Further down towards the end of the room, Alex could see a larger ship sitting in a bay of its own near the hangar doors. It was larger than any of the others and clearly of Vrexen design even though it lacked any of Star's organic components. Alex recognised it as the craft he had seen in the sky when he was abducted driving home late at night on the North Yorkshire Moors.

Entering and exiting the atmospheres of so many planets over the years, the hull had become scarred and weathered, clearly showing a lack of proper care. The sight of the ship that had inflicted such terror on him in that first encounter now just elicited a kind of sadness for all of those wasted lives. As he turned away from the Vrexen vessel, something caught his eye at the far side of the room. Heart racing, Alex jogged down the line of ships, disbelief clear on his face.

There, tucked away in the corner of the vast room, stood his car. The old Ford Focus looked incredibly out of place surrounded by all the various spacecraft and the awe Alex had felt when entering the room was quickly replaced with a pang of homesickness at the familiar sight. The hood stood wide open, and he was dismayed to see that there was no engine inside. It took him a moment to realise he probably wouldn't ever drive it again anyway, but the reliable machine had given him a touch of freedom, both when he injured his back and when he had moved back up north where a car was essential.

He tested the handle and, surprisingly, found the door unlocked. Leaning inside, he opened the glove compartment only to find it too was empty. Once he had confirmed that the boot had also been scrubbed of any personal items, he gently closed the door and turned back to continue exploring.

5.15 Ship Hours

"I swear to the 96 cousins, if he doesn't stop circling my head, I will melt him down and turn him into a frying pan!"

"Calm down J, he's just excited." Shanice tried to explain, her point somewhat overshadowed by having to duck as Buddy span in the air overhead.

J'Coub sniffed in annoyance. "Please go and be excited somewhere else! I am trying to do an audit of which supplies we can reproduce on-ship and which will need to be brought in. You will be the one to blame if everyone is forced to go back to eating the slime again!"

Buddy slowed down in the air, then projected '5.14' on the crates next to them and beeped loudly and insistently.

"Shanice, please, can you find something for him to do, preferably at the far end of the ship?"

Shanice raised her hand and took hold of one of the little beings' arms. "Come on Buddy. Let's go find something for you to take apart and put back together again, even better."

Buddy turned his blue eye on her and whistled dubiously.

"I'm sure we can find something weird for you to poke at. Maybe we can convince Star to let us give her a makeover?"

A voice rang through the cargo bar. "I poisoned one crew Shanice and I can do it again." Buddy let out a querulous buzz before Star continued. "However, Omni and I do think we might be able to squeeze another 0.7% efficiency from the heat retention systems. It appears you did not calibrate them properly when you made your last set of repairs."

The floating droid shot upwards in indignation, made a vulgar sound and shot off towards the offending systems.

2.17 Ship Hours

The crew sat on Star's Bridge, staring at the screen ahead of them. Shanice hummed to herself whilst Sorah sat rigidly upright.

Alex and J'Coub were sitting at the holo table, trying to agree on the rules of a card game they had invented.

Anticipation had long since turned to boredom, as they waited to be in visual range of the mega structure. Even Buddy had uncharacteristically settled on the floor of The Bridge, one crab idly nipping at his torso as The Engineer scanned his own hands one by one.

It was when J'Coub and Sorah joined in on Shanice's humming that Star quietly turned off her audio sensors in that room.

14. Mega Structure

"We are coming into visual range of the Mega structure now. If you please take notice of the viewing screen, I will enhance the image for you." Star's voice cut through the quiet on The Bridge.

Immediately, the crew jumped to attention, even the few who had drifted off into a gentle sleep. The excitement was palpable as the image slowly came into focus, but nobody dared speak.

At first, they saw a dark orb, glowing ever so slightly with an oily, iridescent sheen. But as they flew closer, the image came into greater detail and the vastness of the construction took the crew's collective breath away. Whatever it was, it surrounded whatever star lay at the centre of the system entirely. What first appeared to be a smooth structure became more defined and huge planet sized hexagonal panels came into view along the inner hull. The whole thing was almost too vast to comprehend and soon Star was dwarfed by the immense object, even though they were still relatively far away.

"I can't believe what I am seeing. That thing is impossible! How did anyone ever construct that?" Alex gasped in awe.

Buddy made a long, low whistle and floated closer to the screen. Soon, the massive sphere took up the entire viewscreen and still it kept on growing. More and more details came into view. Details and measurements on scales the team had never even heard of flashed across their visors and Alex felt a coldness in the pit of his stomach when he realised that even the gaps at the edges of the hexagons were hundreds of miles across.

Closer and closer Star flew, and the crew began to make out continent sized constructs on the outer hull, still sparking with light even after being abandoned for so long. Sorah, exhilarated, stood, and she leant forward on the table.

Star's voice echoed from her wall once again. "Although none of my kind has ever been inside, I am aware of several places where it will be possible to do so. I have plotted a course for one of these."

Still, silence reigned inside The Bridge. Shanice gripped the edge of her chair as she stared ahead. The endless hull of the mysterious sphere expanded further on the screen and they could now make out a hexagonal opening ahead of them. Light from the sun inside spilled out slightly, but looked far dimmer than they would expect.

Only as they got closer did they realise that the opening wasn't a clear gap but had another layer miles inside to ensure that the sphere captured as much of the star's energy as possible. It was much more manageable and the dimensions only seemed grand, rather than vast.

Star's engines hummed louder as the gravity of the sphere affected her. Although she had been here before with others of her kind, she had never come so close. Despite her years of travelling through space and seeing what the universe offered, she had never felt so small and insignificant as she did now.

"Here we go." J'Coub said reverently. "Lets see what's inside this baby."

Star entered the gap in the hull. The surrounding walls somehow made the size of the object seem smaller as she passed through, but it still took long, inexorable minutes for them to clear the passageway and turn past the inner shield.

The light of the captive sun grew brighter and finally they emerged into the interior of the Mega Structure. The walls inside looked spotted at first, but as they drifted past, they could see they were actually burn marks inside the hexagonal shapes, much smaller than those on the outside but some several miles wide and others immense.

"What the fuck?" Alex exclaimed as Star turned towards the centre of the sphere. "It's empty?"

Aside from the star glowing brightly in the centre of the vast space, there was nothing to be seen between it the walls themselves.

"Why would someone build something like this and just leave it empty?" Sorah asked.

J'Coub couldn't take his eyes off the screen, his previous sense of foreboding replaced with an almost crushing disappointment. "Maybe it wasn't built to live in, but for some other reason? Power generation for something else?"

"Despite appearances, I am detecting multiple objects within the sphere. There seems to be a multitude of small linear acceleration devices which look like they were used to make navigation within the Sphere quicker. There are also two larger objects within the perimeter of the construct." Star reported. "There is a protrusion on one section against the wall approximately 1.57AU from our current location. Additionally, there appears to be a small artificial moon, 1AU away from the star in heliocentric orbit within the Sphere. It is currently in a position of opposition, directly across the sun from us."

"It's where? In what orbit?" Shanice asked.

Understanding dawned on Alex. "I get it. It's behind the sun at the moment, hence why we can't see it. We are at 6 and the moon is at 12 if the star was the centre of a clock. Um, except the clock is a ball." He paused. "Know what I mean?"

"Primatives." J'Coub joked. "So hey, it's a bit of a letdown. It doesn't change why we are here. Which one should we check out first? Buddy?"

The Engineer hummed thoughtfully to itself before activating the holo-table to display an image of the wall of the sphere.

Alex nodded at him. "Ok, closest first. Star, can you take us to the protrusion, please?" He eased back into his chair. "Let's see if we can make sense of this place."

"Setting course now, Captain. I am going to use one of the linear accelerators to reduce transit time. Please take your seats and make sure you are secure."

The crew did as requested as the living ship flew gracefully across the interior of the sphere, engines burning high as she picked up speed. They could see the small accelerator on the screen now, a small gateway hanging in space. As Star approached it, lights flickered on around its edges. With one last burn of her engines, Star entered the accelerator and a momentary sensation of weightlessness permeated the ship.

Suddenly, Star hurtled forward through space at almost impossible speeds and the visible wall of the sphere blurred. For several seconds, the crew held their breath, expecting to feel the effects of the abrupt acceleration. When it became apparent that no harm was being done, they settled in to enjoy the journey, but as quickly as it began, they came to an almost full stop upon reaching another hanging gateway.

As they took a moment to orient themselves again, Star continued forward and angled herself towards their destination. Standing out amongst the multitude of hexagonal scars along the wall was a relatively small dome of glass and metal.

"What is it?" Sorah asked as she peered towards the screen, her voice tinged with caution.

J'Coub tapped the screen on his station. "Running a full analysis now, but initial scans show it's a huge habitat. Basically, a city attached to the inner wall of the sphere."

"It looks like smaller than the other burned hexagons." Shanice asked, staring intently at the dome.

Buddy zipped towards the holo-table and projected an image in the centre. A beautifully rendered recreation of the inside of the sphere appeared, with countless glass domes filling it completely. As they watched, each section separated from the wall as enormous engines engaged, pushing them inwards and through the accelerators towards the exit. They left in clusters and singles until all that remained was the single city.

"So they all left then?" Alex asked. The little robot raised its shoulder flaps in an approximation of a shrug. "Ah, it's a theory. Ok. J, what do scans show?"

"Yes, those burn marks could indeed have been made by engines of some sort, for sure. The city itself looks intact, the dome is sealed and…yes…there is a breathable atmosphere. No signs of life that the sensors can recognise, though." He replied.

Alex contemplated the city before him. "Is there anywhere that Star could safely dock?"

"Let me check," Star responded, her voice conveying a hint of curiosity. The screen displayed various points around the dome, highlighting potential docking areas. "There are multiple access points, but the easiest seems to be in the upper hemisphere. It has an airlock system and looks to be the main entrance."

"Then let's head there," Alex decided, his tone firm but filled with an undercurrent of excitement. As Star manoeuvred towards the designated docking area, the crew watched in silence, each lost in their own thoughts about the abandoned city.

The dome grew larger and more detailed as they approached. The glass sections reflected the light of the sun, creating a kaleidoscope of colours on the metal frame in stark contrast to the burn marks around them. It was a breathtaking sight.

Star positioned herself gently against the airlock, the connection seamless. "We made a successful docking," she announced. "I recommend extreme caution. I do not know what you might find inside."

Alex turned to his team, his eyes reflecting the gravity of the moment. "This is uncharted territory," he began, his voice steady. "We need to be prepared for anything. Stay in constant communication, and if anyone feels uncomfortable or in danger, we retreat immediately. We're here to explore and learn, not to take unnecessary risks. Sorah, grab something defensive from the armoury and take point."

Sorah nodded sharply and headed off the bridge. "Shanice, Sorah, Buddy," Alex looked at the trio. "Take anything you need and meet me at the airlock. We need to get as many scans as we can to learn about this place."

As the rest of the crew left The Bridge, Alex spoke to Star. "Star, I'm not expecting trouble, but if anything goes wrong, break the dome and come get us. Our suits should auto engage the helmets. Worse comes to worst, and this is a standing order. Get the hell out of here and protect yourself at all costs. Is that understood?"

"Yes, Captain," Star replied gently. "I will do so at my discretion if there is no other option."

Taking a moment to assess her response, he nodded and headed towards the airlock.

15. The City

Sorah finally joined the rest of the team at the airlock. She quickly went to each of them and attached one of the stun devices she had found earlier to their right wrists, mirroring the data pad on their left. "These have been configured to patch into your suits, so you only need to point two fingers to shoot them. It links with your visors to engage a target to prevent accidental discharge. I have set them to a fairly low level discharge initially, but you can up the voltage with a swipe here." She indicated to a panel on the weapon.

"I see you saved the big gun for yourself. Anyone would think you were overcompensating for something." J'Coub smirked, eyeing the sleek rifle strapped to her back.

Sorah rolled her eyes at him. "Yes, I am overcompensating for a deficiency. A deficiency called J'Coub."

"Ouch. The burns aren't all on the wall outside!" Shanice joked, high fiveing Sorah as she said it.

"Enough team. Let's try to get through this with at least our pride intact." Alex ordered them, turning to face the exit. "Star, if you could open the airlock, please?"

As the airlock doors hissed open, a sense of history and mystery enveloped them. The corridor beyond was dimly lit, the only illumination coming from their suit lights, and the faint glow of dormant technology within the city. Buddy immediately activated a high beam light from the top of his body, illuminating the scene further.

Shanice scanned the area and nodded, deactivating her helmet so only the visor remained. The air was stale but breathable, a testament to the lasting efficiency of the city's life support systems.

They moved forward cautiously, their footsteps echoing in the silent passageway. Slowly, the light grew brighter as they neared the exit, and the sun's radiance illuminated the space beyond. Buddy whizzed along, scanning the walls of the tunnel whilst the other four could not help but look ahead.

Suddenly, they emerged into a wide circular plaza surrounded by lush, overgrown greenery in raised beds surrounding the space. Towering plants stretched up towards the dome, 20 or thirty metres high as soft white vines stretched from tree to tree.

"Wow!" Shanice's mouth hung open as she stopped in her tracks to stare. "Uh. Wow!"

J'Coub looked awed as he took in the vista. "It's beautiful. I can't believe the flora is doing so well if it has been abandoned as long as Star says. It must have some kind of automated process in place. I notice that the plaza at least does not have a buildup of detritus, so something bust be keeping the place clean."

Alex had also noticed that despite the long abandonment, the infrastructure at least looked almost new. If it wasn't for the deathly silence that permeated the place and the stale smell in the air, he could imagine it was abandoned only yesterday. "Buddy," He turned to their technological friend. "Fancy flying higher to get a good look ahead?"

Buddy chirped in acknowledgement and small thrusters materialised from his nano-tech body before igniting and lifting the droid above the tree line.

"Look, you can see the city beyond these trees." Sorah pointed through a gap in the large plants around them. Through the greenery, they could see a variety of buildings towering in the distance. Huge teardrop shaped towers rose up, their delicate points glimmering in the sunlight. Sorah could see a variety of sizes and shapes, some smooth and reflecting those around them and others etched in meticulous honeycomb patterns, forming an outer layer through whose gaps you could see their central cores.

Alex used his visor to enhance his view and whistled appreciatively. "They really love their Hexagons. This place almost feels like the people only vanished 5 minutes ago."

Threaded between the buildings, endless metal pipelines seemed to stretch, reminding Alex of a monorail, but dotted along them and from balconies, more greenery grew, vibrant and bright against the silver metals. In places, this draped down to the floor or stretched from building to building.

As they looked at the cityscape, Buddy started relaying aerial images down to their Visors along with a rudimentary map of the areas he had scanned. From above, the city looked like a complex geometric pattern of hexagons and triangular parks or plazas in between them. Snaked between them all were the mysterious pipes. Occasionally some of the hexagonal sections merged together and larger buildings filled those spaces, giant spherical structures or complex clusters of rings and domes.

Sorah tapped her arm pad, downloading the data to her own personal filing system. "What's the plan Captain?" She asked Alex.

"I think we let Buddy complete the arial scans, then he can identify points of interest for either him or us to explore. Target wise, we have a twofold strategy. We need to identify any technology or materials we can use to upgrade Star to give us a fighting chance against The Divinium or The Vrexen, be that offensive, defensive or otherwise. Second, we should find as much about the creators of this place as possible. Any information we get is going to be valuable." He explained to the team. "Finally, it's unlikely, but if we can find anything we can use as supplies that haven't long rotted away, it will save us a detour down the line."

"Understood, Captain." Sorah adjusted the rifle on her back for comfort. She remained alert, but her posture had relaxed slightly. "I think we should stay together, at least at first. We can always split up once we have more detailed readings of the place. I don't think we are in danger, but I would rather to be sure."

"Yeah, I'm SO not splitting up. Every sci-fi film I have ever seen says that is a bad idea." Shanice interjected as she sidled closer to Sorah, her eyes darting to the dense bushes around them. The musty air was warm as she inhaled and she could smell the surrounding plants, a heady wood like aroma. "Maybe in, like, a year when we are all used to this shit."

Alex barked out a laugh. "Sure, we stick together for now, aside from Buddy. Just nobody touch any weird eggs." He took a quick look around and pointed towards a pathway through the trees. "Ok, let's head out. Keep your eyes open and stay together."

The group set a steady pace towards the city, J'Coub whistling quietly as he went. As they broke through the tree line, the city proper came into full view. Strange sculptures stood at either end of the pathway, framing the exit from the plaza. Made from an iridescent metal, interlocking rings and bars surrounded a tall thin central column inscribed with crescent moons and what looked like a representation of a vinelike plant.

Beyond the sculptures, the first of the buildings were even more impressive up close. A thoroughfare led between two enormous towers, the floor covered with pathways, greenery and a small stream. The building to their right was one of the towering teardrop towers, an oily rainbow sheen faintly patterning its surface whilst the leftmost building was a cylindrical tower with a dimpled skin as if a giant had meticulously pressed thumbprints into soft clay.

The gentle sound of the flowing water was the only noise they could hear as they walked across the street. J'Coub looked towards his teammates. "How do we choose where to explore? I can't see a way of telling what these places even are?"

"I think just trial and error, to be honest." Alex replied with a shrug. "Until we learn more about the people that lived here or until Buddy can give us some direction, let's just explore. Let's hit the one on the right first." Alex casually pointed to the tall tear-drop shaped building and cocked his head towards it. "Let go!"

The four moved towards the building at a casual pace, their eyes belaying the relaxed nature of their movements, carefully scanning the surroundings as they passed. Looming above them, the tower stood sleek and elegant and the arch of the doorway lay ahead. None of them could recognise the swooping elegant script inscribed on the smooth surface of the door.

"Uploading the scans to Buddy." J'Coub was tapping away on his wrist pad. "Translators aren't working on this language, so we will need a lot more data before we can start decoding it. Buddy, how are you doing up there?"

An imitation of a wolf whistle rang through their internal comm units and the map on their Visors updated. Hundreds of green dots appeared all over the map where Buddy had labelled points of interest for them.

Alex took in the vast amount of information on his screen. "Great job Buddy. Log them all and see if you can narrow things down for us a bit. Feel free to join us whenever you are ready."

A whistle acknowledged him and the comms went quiet as Alex approached the door, looking for a way to open it. He tentatively ran his hand down the inscribed script, admiring the handiwork. Pushing on the door yielded nothing and there didn't appear to be any controls nearby."Any ideas?" He asked his team?

"I can try to blow a hole in it?." Sorah suggested, touching the rifle on her shoulder.

Alex put a hand on her arm. "Last resort Sorah. Anyone else?"

"Maybe this one is just locked and we can try the other one first?" J'Coub suggested.

"Open Sesame?" Shanice shouted, waving her arms in front of the closed door to no effect.

The group shared a brief chuckle at Shanice's attempt before turning their attention back to the problem at hand. Just then, Buddy's high-pitched chirp sounded over their comm units and a glowing square appeared on their HUDs, drawing their attention to a small panel hidden in the shadows to the side of the door.

"Buddy found something!" Alex exclaimed as they gathered around the panel. It was sleek and undecorated, blending almost seamlessly with the wall. A series of unfamiliar symbols glowed faintly on its surface.

"Let's see if it's some kind of control panel," J'Coub suggested, reaching out to touch the symbols. As his fingers brushed against them, the symbols changed colour, cycling through a spectrum of hues before settling on a bright blue. The door let out a low hum and slowly slid open, revealing the interior of the teardrop tower.

Inside, a vast, open space greeted them. The architecture was fluid, with curved walls that rose up to form an intricate lattice pattern on the ceiling. Soft lights gently flicked on, filtering in from above, casting a serene glow on the entire area. A mosaic of tiles covered the floor, with each tile slightly raised and gently depressing as they walked over them.

"Look at this," Shanice said, pointing to a mural on one wall. It depicted a stylised view of the city in pale, muted colours.

"Interesting," Sorah mused, examining the mural closely. "Is it utilitarian or is it art? J?"

J'Coub studied the image on the wall. "I'd say a mixture of both. It's an accurate representation from what we have seen so far, but is definitely presented artistically. Based on the prominent location in the room and the building's proximity to the Air lock, I'd say this may have been some kind of Welcome Building potentially."

As they ventured deeper into the building, they came across what appeared to be a public gathering space. Circular seating areas were interspersed with lush green plants, and in the centre, a tranquil water feature bubbled softly.

"It certainly feels like a public space rather than a private building." Alex observed, his voice low in reverence.

"It's all so well-preserved," Shanice added, examining a device that looked like a terminal. "There's power still running through here. This city might have been left behind, but it doesn't look like it was abandoned in haste or in chaos. My scans have found no organic life aside from the plants. Or organic remains, for that matter. "

Suddenly the terminal she was examining sparked into full life and a bright sphere of light pulsed through the room, bouncing off the walls and retracting back into the terminal.

"I didn't touch anything!" Shanice exclaimed as a holographic image appeared above the terminal. "Wait, is that us?"

The image on the screen was of the four of them exiting from the tunnel, Buddy hovering above them. They watched the image intensely as Buddy shot off in the air to scan the city from above, and the four of them explored the plaza.

"This is so creepy. This was just minutes ago." Shanice observed, watching as the image cut to the quartet entering the very building they were in now. "Why is it showing us this?"

The image focused in on a view of them in this very room right now. Alex, Shanice and J'Coub staring at the image whist Sorah was scanning the room, looking for the viewpoint on the screen. "I cannot see anything that looks like a camera, Captain." She said, and both she and the image on the projection turned back to face the same direction.

The image on the screen flickered and the four representations of the team turned to face them, slowly raising a hand in greeting.

"ooooh that IS creepy" J'Coub shivered as he watched himself on screen, the perfect recreation now acting on its own. "I look great, though."

Alex watched the screen intently, then raised his hand and waved in greeting. "Hello, my name is Alex." He said.

The screen flickered again, and the representation of Alex lowered its arm. The other three continued to wave until, one by one, the team mimicked Alex and introduced themselves. Then the figures on the screen shimmered again and began to transform. Their features became less defined, morphing into more generic, androgynous forms. Then these forms merged into one softly glowing figure.

"Yana." a crisp robotic voice emerged from the screen in front of them. The figure pointed at itself.

Alex looked around at his team curiously and turned back to address the figure. "Pleasure to meet you, Yana. Can you tell me more about this place?"

The image flickered again. Then raised its arms wide and vanished, leaving only the image of the room behind.

The four of them stood in silence, the emotions in the room running high. Slowly the image of the room displayed zoomed out, showing the outside of the building, then panned back even further to show an aerial view of the city. A small dot slowly moved around the projection. A representation of Buddy, they guessed. The image zoomed in again until it showed a spherical building towards the centre of the metropolis. Slowly, the viewpoint lowered until a gigantic door was displayed in the front. Another flicker and suddenly they saw themselves stood in front of the building, pointing towards the door before the projection went dark.

"Sooooo…" Shanice spun on one heel to face Alex. "I'm going to go out on a limb here and suggest it want's us to go there?"

J'Coub stared at her. "Your powers of deduction never cease to amaze me, Shanice."

"How do we feel about this?" Alex asked them. "Buddy, we need you down here with us. I hope you were tuned into our streams there?"

The little AI Being acknowledged him and began to head in their direction. Alex turned to his team.

"Well, we have blundered into this pretty openly so far and although it's all a bit weird, I don't see why we stop now." J'Coub responded first.

Sorah nodded at him, her sharp horns catching the light of the room. "If there is harm intended to us, that was rather a polite way of inviting us to our doom."

"Cheerful!" Shanice said. "Ok, let's head out and meet Buddy on our way." She turned back towards the way out. "I want to take some plant cuttings along the way anyway, and maybe some water samples." She pulled some of the clear sample tubes from her pack.

"OK, let's go then." Alex took the lead and led the team back out of the building. "Star, everything ok over there with you?"

The ship's voice crackled over the comms. "Indeed, Captain. I am availing myself of the resources in the docking bay. Some facilities here for refuelling and resupply of raw materials still have some viable substances we can utilise."

"Great work Star." Alex responded. "I'm just curious. How come your people have visited here before but never been inside?"

"You must understand, Captain, that although my race is sentient, it is not in the same way you would understand. Until I was linked with Omni and spent centuries adapting and learning, many of our motivations were instinctive. We migrated from system to system in a grand progression, each stop for a different purpose. To feed, to mate, to birth, to share information, to grieve and to sing." Star's voice was wistful over the comms. "We gloried in the journey, finishing the progression and starting it again. This stop on our route was traditionally for birthing. We had no reason to go inside, for that would not have been our purpose here."

"I see," Alex replied thoughtfully. "So if we met another of your kind, we could not communicate with them as we do with you?"

"No Captain. They would have no interest in communicating outside their pod, except with another pod. I fear they would not even see me as a sister anymore and my heart tells me I could no longer sing with them either."

There was a moment's silence as the team exited the building and absorbed Star's words. "Then let us look forward instead of backwards." Sorah's voice was firm and warm. "I see you as sister now, Star. Let us create our own songs and journeys together."

"Your words are most kind, Sorah." Star responded quietly.

"Thank you Star. I hope it isn't painful bringing us here."Just let us know if it's a painful memory." Shanice added.

"I do not feel pain here, Shanice. It is simply a place for us to hide, heal, and prepare. But unlike my past self, I am watching through the visors with curiosity."

"Then let's get to that sphere and see what we can uncover." Alex stated firmly and turned down the street to lead the way.

16. The Sphere

Buddy descended from the skies, whistling as he rejoined the team. Shanice was carefully collecting samples from the various plants they saw along the way while J'Coub peered intently inside every window or door they came across.

"I have seen nothing that resembles a shop, bar, or restaurant so far." He observed as they walked. "Unusual for a city of any kind, but even stranger when they had a visitor centre, so obviously had or intended to have some kind of tourism or visitation."

Alex was going through some data that Buddy had gained on his visor. "Agreed, although it is possible they are centralised in another district. Do you think each of those burned hexagons on the walls outside was a city of its own?"

"Possibly." J'Coub replied. "Hard to tell, as this is the only surviving example and they vary so much in size. It could have been thousands of duplicates of this one, or they could have all had different purposes, designs, or even be from different species. Anything is possible, I guess."

"Sphere should be just around the next corner," Sorah, who had taken point again, pointed out. "Buddy, welcome back, friend. Sorry we dragged you back down, but we thought you would want to see this."

Buddy beeped in acknowledgement and floated next to Sorah, scanning the street as they reached the junction.

Turning the corner, a spectacular sight greeted them. A vast sphere hovered above the ground, floating on a soft green column of light. Glittering raised silver designs covered its surface, resembling the alien script the crew had seen before. Buddy immediately took to the air to scan the sphere in its entirety.

As Buddy whirled around it, mapping every inch, the team approached cautiously, their eyes fixed on the floating marvel.

"Looks like this might be some sort of central hub building or landmark," Alex speculated, his gaze following Buddy's flight path.

Shanice, still clutching her sample tubes, looked up in awe. "It's like something out of a dream. Do you think we can get inside?"

J'Coub, who had been quiet, finally spoke up. "The design, the way it's suspended... it's too deliberate to be just decorative. There has to be a purpose to it."

Sorah examined the green column of light. "This doesn't seem to be just a support beam. It could be for energy or data transfer. Maybe it's powering the sphere or even getting power from the sphere?"

As they neared the base of the sphere, a panel on its surface began to glow brighter, responding to their presence. The designs around the panel shifted, forming what looked like an entrance.

Buddy completed his scan and descended back to the group, projecting a detailed 3D model of the sphere onto their visors. "Looks like we have a way in," Sorah noted, gesturing towards the glowing panel.

Alex nodded. "Alright, let's proceed, but stay alert. We don't know what we might find inside."

The team cautiously approached the glowing panel. As they got closer, the panel slid open silently, revealing a dark interior, and a ramp descended to ground level. They hesitated for a moment before stepping inside, their suits' lights automatically activating to illuminate the surrounding space.

"Am I the only one that hoped we were going to get 'beamed aboard'?" Alex joked.

"Wait! How can we have been in space this long and we haven't teleported anywhere?" Shanice joked, trying to break the tension.

Sorah looked at her strangely. "Was Star moving between solar systems not enough for you?"

"Quiet guys. We need to stay alert." Alex motioned for them to quieten them down as they moved through the dark space. The team instinctively huddled closer together as their lights illuminated the smooth tunnel as they walked down.

Buddy chirped quietly as his blue scan beam lit up the space ahead, revealing an archway into a large space ahead. As soon as the team breached the threshold of this space, a warm light glowed. An enormous ball of light appeared levitating in the centre of the room, flooding the room with heat and bringing the space into crisp clarity.

"It's the mega structure!" Shanice exclaimed in wonder as she stared around the space. "That ball of light is the star in the centre."

"Look. Theres the City we are in over here." J'Coub pointed as he walked around the space. "Fascinating. I wonder if this is a live image?"

"Where's the moon?" Alex asked. "Over the other side of the sun? J'Coub, can you see it?"

J'Coub's voice echoed from the walls as he responded. "I can indeed, Alex. You should come see this. That's no moon."

The team all moved quickly to J'Coubs position.

"Pleasedontbeadeathstar" Shanice muttered under her breath as she went.

There, hanging in the air orbiting the sun, was the moon. Or rather, artificial moon, because the object they saw was far from natural. In front of them was a huge cube floating in the air, spinning slowly on its points. Gleaming white in the light from the sun, hundreds of thousands of spires dotted its surface in a tight grid.

Buddy scanned the moon and floated up to it, chittering excitedly as he extended a manipulator arm towards it. With a gesture, he swiped across the cube and the image vanished and reappeared in the centre of the room, replacing the Star.

"Jesus, Buddy, give me a heads up if you are going to do that." Shanice had literally jumped when the room changed suddenly. Alex, Sorah and J'Coub had fared little better at the surprise, but soon became fascinated by the enlarged image.

"This place must be some kind of observatory, or control room maybe?" Alex observed as he studied the cube. "Can we see the surface please, Buddy?"

The Engineer made a series of complicated gestures and the image zoomed in further. The spires were immense, each identical to the other.

"Odd, I wonder what they were for. Buddy, can you zoom in closer on one, please?"

One tower filled the room, gleaming white. The team could now make out more of that now familiar glittering script, but covering every inch of the spire. There appeared to be no doors or windows anywhere, just writing from top to bottom.

"Is it a library? A museum?" Shanice asked curiously.

"It could be artwork, or a warning of some kind, possibly?" J'Coub postulated.

Buddy zipped upwards almost into the image itself, scanning the text furiously and manipulating the projection to scroll from spire to spire. The crew's visors flickered as he transferred an incredible amount of information through them to Star and Omni. As quick as it happened, he stopped and made a low whine, rotating slowly to face the crew.

"What? What is it?" Alex asked cautiously.

"Alex." Star's voice came through the comms. "It will take some time to translate this language fully, but based on syntax and some initial observations, this appears to be a list of names and dates. My best guess as to the purpose of the cube is that it is a memorial of some kind."

"My God. There must be hundreds of thousands of names there." Shanice wrapped her arms around herself.

"Many, many millions." J'Coub said quietly. "Looking at the initial scans Buddy sent, it appears they were all inscribed around the same time."

A reverential silence filled the room as everyone took time to absorb the magnitude of what that meant.

Slowly, the image faded as Buddy interfaced with the system once again. The walls shimmered with light and rippled as the projection changed. Where there had once been a single city pod, the sphere was now covered with them, all varying wildly in size, the city being one of the smallest by far.

"Incredible!" J'Coub whispered as he moved to examine them further. "They have some similarities, but each dome is different. Cities, oceans, forests. So many biomes. Some of these are the size of a large planet!"

"Here!" Sorah shouted as the team turned towards her. Limping into the space, a ship appeared. It was obvious that the ship was badly damaged and barely holding itself together as it slowly made its way forward. A white orb appeared in front of the battered craft and began to tow it towards one biome. More orbs appeared and ship after ship were slowly escorted to different locations. Most of the ships looked to be of vastly different designs, and all were in various states of damage.

Now the space is full of ships, all being escorted to their designated biomes. "It's an Ark. On an unimaginable scale." Alex felt a chill run down his spine. "What could have caused a disaster that affected so many races?"

Sorah looked pale. "War." She touched her chest in a reverential gesture. "Those are the scars of battle, and these ships all arrive together. They appear to be different races, different classes and hardly any built for war."

"Refugees from thousands and thousands of worlds. Assuming they are from this sector, why have none of us ever heard of this? Star, do you have any records?"

"I have nothing in our databases that matches the visuals of these ships." Star said. "It is possible that if Buddy accesses their database, I can make a more thorough analysis."

"So each ark looks custom made for each species. Why is this city still here?" J'Coub ran his fingers through the glittering hologram.

"They never made it here." Alex suggested. "Maybe nobody from that race survived, and the city has been sitting empty ever since. It would make sense, as we haven't found any traces of life so far. It's thousands of years old at least, maintained by some kind of advanced systems, but essentially untouched and unused."

Buddy manipulated the image again and the remembrance moon span faster and faster as the years passes, occasionally lights flickered across the space as ships travelled from Ark to Ark. Inside the biomes seasons passed in seconds and civilisations flourished and then the image slowed and the Arks, one by one, launched from the walls of the sphere, out the way they came until only their city was left and the image faded.

The sphere was dark again, illuminated only by their suit lights. Across their visors, Buddy projected some figures. "Ok, looks like there were 402,765 Unique Habitats across this space and they were inhabited for approximately 217 rotations around the sun." Shanice read aloud to the group. "Nothing about why they all left again at the same time. It must have been an incredible effort to coordinate so many civilisations."

With the warmth from the simulated star now gone, the space felt cold and oppressive. Heavy with the weight of the history, they had learned the team looked around the space one more time before heading back towards the door. Outside in the sun's warmth, the city nevertheless felt quiet and still.

Alex led the team to a low wall outside beside a small stream running along one edge of the Sphere Plaza and gestured for them all to sit. "Lets take 5 so we can gather our thoughts here. That was a lot."

"Yeah. You can say that again." Shanice sighed as she sat down. "I can barely comprehend the scale involved, and this was what? Thousands of years ago?"

J'Coub crouched down and ran his hand idly through the water. "At least. Who is to say that the descendents of those involved even know what happened here? It may just be stories to them, broken, forgotten and mistranslated through the generations."

Sorah leant back against a tree, arching her back against it revelling in the feel of the wood against her. "I feel the weight of what we have learned. This event must be remembered and we should find out all we can, but soon we need to focus on our primary mission. We have not been together long and already two entire races hate us and we know of an ancient tragedy that nobody else knows of. My people have a saying, 'When the eyes of the forest are all upon you, you either walk into scared ground or into their stomachs.'"

"Yeah, maybe I will end up going home after all." Shanice deadpanned, her gaze lost in the stream.

As the group sat in silence, each lost in their own thoughts, Buddy's soft electronic whirring broke the quiet. The AI floated towards them, a soft glow emanating from his core. "Alex," Star's voice was unusually sombre over the comms, "Buddy has been scanning the substructures of the city. There's something beneath you, a network of chambers and tunnels. The race that built this mega structure may have left resources for the people who were supposed to inhabit this city."

Alex perked up at this information. "Resources? What kind of resources?"

"Unknown," Star replied. "But the preliminary scans suggest advanced materials, possibly similar to the ones used in his construction. Exploring these chambers could yield vital resources."

J'Coub looked up, his interest piqued. "This could be a significant find. If these materials are advanced nanites like Buddy's, imagine what we could do with them."

Sorah stood up, brushing the bark from her back. "It feels like a path is unfolding before us. Perhaps our journey here isn't just about survival but about discovery, too."

Shanice stood up slowly, her expression resolute. "OK, you guys go ahead. I'm going to head back to Star to analyse these samples."

"You need to pee, don't you?" Sorah knew her roommate better than anyone.

"AND analyse the samples. That ok Alex?" she queried.

"Sure. But you know you can pee in your suit right, it absorbs.."

"NOPE. Not there yet. Space I can handle, abandoned cities fine, but peeing my pants? Step too far and you DARE tell me how the ship recycles water and I will turn your vocal cords off next time you are in Med Bay."

Alex held his hands up in surrender. "Fine, off you go and try not to think of all the streams and waterfalls running along the way back." He smiled.

Shanice was already moving away, back toward the docking area. "Hate you, bye!"

Alex turned to the rest of them, feeling the weight of curiosity settle upon him. "Buddy, lead the way. Let's see what secrets this city holds beneath its silence."

As they followed Buddy towards a hidden entrance, the tranquillity of the plaza was replaced with a sense of purpose. The city, quiet and still, seemed to watch them as they delved deeper into its forgotten layers, ready to reveal its long-held secrets.

17. Running Rings

Shanice walked quickly back along the streets of the city. She was more relaxed in the uninhabited ark now that she understood its history. Somehow, the sense of sorrow from the troubled history had transformed into something peaceful and reflective. Despite her pressing need, she still marvelled at the beauty of the city and how much of it was so vibrant with plant life.

She had seen no sign of any maintenance system keeping the plants from overgrowing and the water ran clear, so upkeep was definitely happening, but how was still a mystery to her. She soon reached the entrance to the plaza where they had originally arrived, and her bladder tingled at the nearness of home.

A cool breeze brushed against her cheeks as she made her way across the plaza towards Star, and she all but jogged through the tunnel to the docking bay and up the ramp. Quickly making her way through the corridors, she found the toilet and breathed a sigh of relief. Sitting there she was relieved in several senses of the word, physically and also glad to be back on Star, where she felt in control of the situation again.

Finishing up, she let the decontamination field from the hygiene unit run across her hands when a sudden, urgent alert from Star abruptly grasped her attention. "Shanice, sensors are detecting incoming objects at high velocity. I believe we are under attack. The Divinium ships have returned."

Her heart pounding, Shanice dashed to the bridge, where the view of the serene city was now marred by the sight of three Divinium ships approaching at a menacing speed from one of the acceleration gates. "How did we not sense them coming?"

"The acceleration gates brought them here faster than my long range sensors could pick them up, I am afraid. What should we do?" Star replied as the various stations on the Bridge activated one by one.

"The others won't make it back in time, and I don't know how well the city dome would hold up to a direct attack." Shanice calculated quickly in her head, briefly hesitating before sitting in the Captain's chair. "Alert the others and disembark one of the ships in the hangar for them, preferably something heavily shielded or armed to the teeth. We need to lure them away from the city for now. Camouflage yourself and let's move out as quietly as we can at first."

Star's voice was calm, yet Shanice could detect a hint of urgency, "Camouflage activated. We are still vastly outgunned, but we will do whatever we can. I am afraid I cannot reach the others. We are being jammed somehow."

The Captain's chair moulded to her body and her Visor synched to the primary control systems. Shanice nodded to herself upon hearing that their comms were down. "Of course they bloody are." She watched as Star stealthily exited the docking bay and used her tentacles to guide herself along the massive sphere's surface to blend with its exterior. The first missile launched from one of the enemy ships and exploded against the city's shield, sending a shockwave that reverberated through the air.

Star manoeuvred skilfully, using the mega-structure's terrain to their advantage. Shanice's mind raced, trying to formulate a strategy to fend off the Divinium ships with guerrilla tactics, utilising the little firepower and agility they had. "Ok, the only benefits we have here are our stealth and close range combat abilities." Shanice said, her voice steady despite the rising adrenaline. "That and we have had more time to understand the scans of this place. I suggest we launch a surprise attack at their missiles and scanners and then use the acceleration network to move away as quickly as possible. Even if they do not all give chase, we can at least get their attention."

Star acknowledged her plan. "I suggest we attack the largest of the three vessels from stealth, with as much firepower as possible. This would be most unexpected. But I must ask Shanice, you seemed much affected by the destruction of the other vessel. Are you sure this is something you wish to pursue?"

Shanice nodded her head firmly. "It really is them or us, Star. After the initial attack, we can broadcast a repeat pre-recorded request for them to leave or surrender. But they give me no choice." She reached down to her console and hit record. "This is Shanice Francis of the independent Vessel Star. Your people have attacked us once already and were destroyed. Leave us alone, return to your space and we will not pursue you. This is your final warning." She finished the recording and set it to send when she hit the button. "Ready Star?"

Star's systems hummed in response, a subtle affirmation of readiness. "I am prepared, Shanice."

With a deep breath, Shanice initiated their stealthy approach. Star glided silently across the expanse of the mega-structure's surface, blending seamlessly with its exterior. As they neared the largest Divinium ship, Shanice's hands were steady on the controls, her focus absolute and no trace of her earlier fear showed..

"Launching a surprise attack in three... two... one... Now!" Shanice commanded, and Star unleashed a volley of whatever armaments she had at her disposal towards the Divinium ship's missile bays and scanners.

The Divinium ship reeled from the unexpected attack, its sensors momentarily blinded. Shanice quickly triggered the pre-recorded message, broadcasting their ultimatum.

Without waiting to see if the Divinium would heed their warning, Shanice directed Star towards the nearest acceleration gate. "Let's move, Star. Use the acceleration network to put some distance between us."

Star surged forward, entering the gate. The sensation of weightlessness filled the vessel as they were hurtled through space at an incredible speed. Shanice kept her eyes glued to the sensors, watching for any signs of pursuit. She was immensely glad she had peed before this all started.

As they emerged from the acceleration gate, Shanice could see that two of the Divinium ships had taken the bait and were following them. "Alright, Star, let's lead them on a chase they won't forget."

The chase was intense, with Star weaving through the structure, narrowly evading the barrage of missiles from their pursuers. Shanice's strategy was working; they were drawing the enemy away from the city and her friends. Jumping from one gate to another with only moments of normal speed in between to launch a defence.

But she knew this couldn't last forever. Eventually, they would have to confront the Divinium head-on. The comms thrummed with a response from one of the Divinium ships. "Abominations, particularly those under the command of a female captain, will not be engaged in negotiations, only cleansed from the cosmos."

Shanice's stare turned cold. "Star, set a course for the nearest Divinium ship. It's time we fight dirty."

As they hurtled towards their first real confrontation, Shanice's grip tightened on the controls, ready to face the challenge head-on. She brought up the chosen ship in the targeting reticule. "I wonder if they know you are female, too?" Shanice grinned. "How about the same tactic as before? Grab and squeeze?"

"With the other vessel so close, we risk being targeted as the attack took some time. However, I suggest a modified approach." Star suggested and relayed her plan to Shanice's visor.

Shanice's grin widened. "Do it. We break off as soon as we can and into the acceleration network. Then we can loop around the sun back to the original ship and assess the damage we did. Be prepared to fire another barrage before we make another circuit. GO!"

Star engaged her Camoflauge again, making her harder to spot as she darted through space towards her target. Once she came into range, she deftly reversed course and released a cloud of nano-particles. This time, however, it was a distraction and not a place to hide. Still camouflaged and with incredible speed, Star shot sideways from the cloud and then adjusted course to head towards her prey.

The manoeuvre bought them vital moments, but the enemy ship still fired several bolts from an energy weapon mounted on her hull, some burning into Star as she attacked. But it was too late. Star wrapped her tentacles around the Divinium ship's hull. She was in too close now.

"NOW Star!" Shanice shouted before her friends more primal instincts cut in. The lights on the Bridge dimmed and flickered back on as Star release one of her natural defences. Blue lightning danced from Star across the enemy ship's hull.

Her bioelectric defence reminded Shanice of the shock from an electric eel, but far more useful as a powerful electromagnetic pulse rippled outwards and the lights on the enemy ship went dark.

Star gently disengaged from her target. They both knew time was of the essence as the other Divinium ship came blasting through the nano-particle cloud in hot pursuit. Star followed the plan and headed towards the next acceleration gate as fast as she could. "Based on previous scans of their vessels and the level of damage done to that ship, they will not regain power for several hours, so now it is two against one." Star informed Shanice.

"Great." She replied, wiping swear from her brow. "Shame we can only use that trick once in a while. Let's go see what damage we did to the previous ship."

The gravity sling took effect and Star shot into space just as the other vessel's missiles would have struck them. The inertia would have been unbearable if they were not protected by the alien technology in the acceleration network. Almost too soon, they were on their way towards the city once more.

"Missiles and rail guns ready." Star announced. "Arriving in 3, 2, 1 NOW!" Suddenly, the enemy craft filled the screen. "Initiating evasive manoeuvres!"

"Bastards realised what we were doing. Firing everything while you dance your dance!" Shanice yelled as she directed all their firepower towards the vessel's engines. Targeting the weapons was impossible from the angle they were approaching, so she made a quick decision and let loose.

Whether by luck or skill, the vast majority of the missiles hit, even as Star performed the kind of space acrobatics that no other craft could perform, but the damage wasn't restricted to the massive battlecruiser. Shockwave after shockwave rippled through Star as missiles exploded against her scale armour.

"Minimal damage, but we have compromised armour in 3 places," Star informed her.

"Noted. What damage did we manage to do to them?" Shanice queried, her fingers dancing across the controls as she reloaded their weapons. "Give me some good news, baby girl!"

"Their engines are badly damaged and they are effectively immobile. However, their weapons remain unaffected and will be drawing power from a separate reactor."

Shanice nodded, expecting as much. "Ok, I don't want to do another run around the structure. I can already see damage on the city dome. We have minutes at the most before the other ship makes it through the acceleration network. How about we use that network as a weapon?"

Star considered this briefly. "Missiles fired into the network could not make the navigational adjustments necessary to do that."

"No, but if we push this engineless ship in front of the exit, RIGHT in front of it. Then we essentially turn the other ship into a massive bullet fired by the network? Would that work?"

"It will work if we move now. We will need to act fast and then withdraw to protect the city from any debris that may be expelled towards it. Moving in towards the ship now."

Shanice focused her eyes on the Divinium vessels damaged stern as Star edged closer, and the strain of the operation became clear in the hum of her engines. "Gently does it.," Shanice muttered to herself, her fingers tapping rhythmically on the control panel. "Star, use your tentacles to latch onto their structural points. It's going to be rough, but hopefully we are shielded from most of their weapons at this angle."

Star's response was a focussed silence, her tentacles extending and wrapping around the Divinium ship. The view outside blurred as Star fired her engines, the immense bulk of the disabled ship resisting movement.

"We're on a tight clock here," Shanice spoke, her voice a mix of urgency and control, broadcasting her instructions over the comm. "I'm bracing for impact and preparing for immediate debris management."

The physical strain on Star was tangible. The ship groaned under the stress, and Shanice could feel the tension vibrating through the floor. "Come on, Star, just a little further, baby girl," she encouraged, her eyes fixed on the navigation screen.

Calculating the trajectory with precision, she guided Star in manoeuvring the Divinium ship towards the acceleration gate. "This has to be exact," she said, her focus unyielding as she eyed the approaching second Divinium ship on the sensors.

The seconds felt like hours as Star, with a last surge of power, positioned the disabled ship directly in front of the acceleration gate exit. "Perfect, Star! Now, pull back!" Shanice commanded, her heart racing.

As they retreated to a safe distance, Shanice could see the second Divinium ship emerging from the acceleration network, barrelling towards the unexpected blockade. The collision was imminent.

"Brace for impact!" she yelled. The moment the two Divinium ships collided, a catastrophic explosion lit up the space, sending shockwaves rippling through the mega-structure. Debris scattered in all directions.

Star skilfully dodged the larger fragments, her movements swift and graceful despite her size. "Several impacts across my hull, damage in some of my lower sections, but monitor that debris heading towards the city," Star informed Shanice, her systems whirring as she multitasked.

Shanice exhaled a deep breath she didn't realise she had been holding. "Great job, Star. Let's assess the damage and try to contact the others." Her voice was firm, but relief tinged her words.

As the dust settled, the city remained untouched, the debris harmlessly drifting away from it. They had successfully protected the ancient mega-structure and its secrets. Shanice allowed herself a moment of pride, feeling the weight of her decisions and their successful execution.

"Let's circle back and check on the team," Shanice decided, her resolve as strong as ever. "Star, set a course. We're not done yet."

18. Engaging the Enemy

"Oh Hey guys." Shanice answered the incoming urgent hail from the team.

"Shanice, thank god!" Alex's voice crackled over the comms, the urgency in his tone clear. "We are just boarding the shuttle you left us. Can you hold on out there? We can see explosions outside the dome, but that's it!"

Shanice chuckled to herself. "Yeah, three Divinium warships attacked us, but Star and I took care of them. No biggie."

"You…took care of them?" She could hear the concern in his voice. "Are you ok? We should be with you in a few minutes. J'Coub is flying and promised he can handle docking a shuttle."

J'Coubs voice sounded indignant as he intruded on the channel. "Hey, just because you two are primitives, it doesn't mean we all are."

Shanice leant back in the chair, feeling the tension slowly release from her muscles. "I'm ok. Genuinely. Star sustained some damage. We have two destroyed enemy vessels, and one disabled ship we need to decide what to do with. I leave that one for you guys, though."

Another brief pause. "Understood. We are on our way with gifts. No need to meet us, be with you asap." The comms clicked off.

"Star, how badly were you hit?" She asked carefully.

"I will need repairs to my hull. A minor breach has been auto sealed, but there is internal damage to several corridors and one of the waste processing areas that will need to be attended to. The crabs are en route now. I am not in pain, if that is what you are asking."

"Ok, nothing we can't deal with. Glad you aren't hurting. You were incredible just now, Star. You really never stop surprising me."

"As were you, Shanice." Her voice filled the room. "It is regrettable that you had to handle the situation without the others. I know our last encounter deeply affected you."

Shanice idly rubbed her arm and looked towards the wall and was silent for a minute before speaking. "It's never going to be easy, Star, and I don't think it should be. But they really didn't give us much choice. It's clear they want us dead and have no interest in talking. We need to survive."

"Then I will mention it no more. But I am always here if you need to talk," Star said gently. "The others have docked now."

Shanice could hear a whirr getting louder and it reached a crescendo as Buddy flew onto The Bridge at extreme speed, chittering wildly. He barrelled towards Shanice, barely breaking in time to avoid hitting her.

"Whoa Buddy! I'm ok!" She held her hands up to show him she was fine and was surprised when the little robot pressed up against her, wrapping its manipulator arms around her. "Oh," Shanice said quietly, lowering her arms and hugging her friend. "I'm glad to see you safe too, Mr."

She was still holding Buddy when Alex, J'Coub, and Sorah raced onto the bridge. Sorah immediately joined the hug, soon joined by the boys. Buddy squawked indignantly at being squashed between everyone and gently hovered up out of the pile, brushing imaginary dirt off of his chassis.

The four of them disentangled, eyeing each other happily as they plied Shanice with questions and she ran through what had happened, much to the amazement of the other three.

"Nice work, Shanice!" Sorah slapped her on the back. "I wish I had thought of throwing one ship into another. Maybe I can try it next time they come for us."

J'Coub tucked a loose strand of his blue hair behind his ear. "Brilliant, using the acceleration gates against them all. Also, disabling the other ship with an EMP. Nice to know that works against other vessels."

Alex grinned at her. "You did a fantastic job. We should go check out the disabled ship soon, but they should be dead in the water for quite a while yet. Want to see what we brought back?"

Shanice clapped her hands with glee, slightly embarrassed by the praise. "oooh presents! Tell me it's chocolate. Or Alien chocolate. Oooh or cheese!"

"Close!" Alex mimicked J'Coubs jazz hands gesture. "Flexium!"

Shanice screwed her nose up. "That sounds totally made up."

Alex deflated slightly. "Well, I chose the name. But it is AWESOME stuff."

J'Coub raised a hand. "I vote Alex will never be allowed to name anything ever again." Shanice and Sorah immediately raised their hands. "Seconded. Passed." He finished smugly.

"Fine!" Alex raised his hand as well. "Kinda agree. BUT this stuff is a game changer. From the info Buddy sent us, this is essentially the stuff Buddy's people used to create their nanites. It's incredibly rare, hence why The Builders are constantly recreating their world from the same materiel and why they have been attacked so many times."

Buddy let out a long squeal and dashed off The Bridge, obviously having forgotten his new toy in his concern for Shanice.

Alex continued. "Essentially, it is the building blocks for programmable matter once mixed with other elements. Buddy uses it to replenish his nanite supply and then weaves the flexium and some of his nanites into any materiel you want. Super tough, conductive and self repairing it can be shaped any way you want. Not only that, because of the nanites in there, it can be re-shaped at will." His eyes practically shone with excitement. "And get this, there is a TON of that stuff down there. The amount we took barely made a dent."

J'Coub jumped in, clearly also excited by their find. "We think each ark had a supply to be used to create anything that was needed for the refugees it took in. The Celestials must have been incredibly advanced to have amassed such a supply."

"The Celestials?" Shanice asked curiously. "Alex again?"

Sorah barked a laugh. "No, we have translated some murals we found under the city and it seems like that is how the unknown creators of this place referred to themselves, or close to it."

"ANYWAY." J'Coub coughed. "We have enough of the stuff to coat Star's hull and tentacles in the shuttle and will head back for more later."

Alex drummed his fingers on the holo-table. "Although that is our next problem. If the Divinium found us here, then they can find the Flexium. We can't allow it to fall into their hands." He turned to Sorah. "We need to get onto that stranded ship and find out how they keep finding us and see what we can do to prevent it. Buddy is already preparing the Flexium for deployment across Star's Hull, with her permission of course. Once he finishes that, the deployment won't take too long at all, so he can continue after we board the enemy ship."

He turned to his Tactical Officer. "Sorah, I am sure your mind is racing already, but we need a plan to get onto that ship as safely as possible, neutralise any hostiles on boards whilst leaving enough alive for us to interrogate and finally give us plenty of time to get into their systems and mine as much data as possible."

Sorah nodded thoughtfully and turned to her station to bring up their scans of the enemy. "I am scanning the wreckage of the two destroyed ships to get an idea of an internal layout. Any information we can find out is going to help."

Alex turned to Shanice. "Shanice, I want you to head down to Med bay to see if there is anything we can introduce to their environmental systems to knock them out. We do not know their biology, so Sorah and Star will scan any bodies they find to give us a heads up."

Finally, he turned to J'Coub. "J, join Buddy and see if he can spare any of the Flexium for us to integrate into our suits. They are fantastic, but not particularly armoured. Any protection we can get is vital if it turns into the four of us against an entire ship."

"Yes Captain." J'Coub twitched as if he wanted to salute, then turned on his heel and went to find Buddy. Shanice stretched as if preparing for a run, then turned to leave.

"Some free advice for you, Captain." She said before leaving.

"Any wisdom gladly received Shan." Alex looked at her earnestly.

"Pee now, there won't be time later." She smirked and left the bridge.

"Captain, I am only detecting eight life signs aboard the Divinium ship." J'Coub stared at his wrist screen in confusion as Star exited the acceleration gate and set a course for the silent vessel. "Based on the scans for the other ships, there should have been a crew of at least a hundred on board."

Alex stretched, still getting used to the thin coating of Flexium they had hurriedly applied to their suits. There was no time for refinement, they could tweak it to their heart's content later on, but for now, the suits had a slight stiffness to them that wasn't there before. The Flexium was dormant in the suit and could harden on impact and absorb any energy that came their way, whether that be kinetic energy from a physical blow or strike, or from an energy weapon. In more dire circumstances, it would flow outwards and form an armoured covering to protect them from assault.

"Their life support systems would have been affected by the EMP, but nothing that would affect them this quickly. There would have been plenty of air for at least a few days." Sorah calculated.

"We will find out soon enough." Alex looked around the Hanger. They were using the same shuttle that Star had left them on the City. An ugly, boxy thing that was essentially an armoured escort vehicle, but it would fit them all in comfortably, including Buddy. The air still smelled stale in the craft as they entered, despite them having used it earlier. Alex sat next to Sorah on a bench against the wall and Shanice and J'Coub sat opposite. Buddy had attached himself magnetically to the deck at the front of the craft and was steering them across towards the stricken craft. Alex observed his team carefully.

Shanice fiddled with the pouches and pockets on a belt she had attached to her uniform, checking and re-checking the various improvised gas grenades she had created with Star's help. Each contained a variety of materials with anaesthetic and sedative properties, designed to subdue any enemies they came across safely, whilst their suit filter protected the team. Even though she had just destroyed two enemy ships in space battle, face-to-face combat was a whole different ball game and she wanted to ensure things went as safely as possible.

Whilst Shanice was obsessively checking her pouches, Sorah sat rigidly upright, staring ahead. She ran countless different tactical scenarios through her mind, using all the knowledge gained by their previous encounters and the scans of the destroyed ships. No trace remained of the frightened young woman she used to be as she prepared for battle.

J'Coub hummed to himself, appearing for all the world as if he were simply travelling for pleasure rather than into the unknown. The only sign he was nervous was the shaking of his knee and the occasional tic of him brushing an imaginary hair off of his shoulder.

Buddy was uncharacteristically silent. He was not happy at the rush job he had done on their armour. His race were artists and perfectionists living a peaceful life on their planet, ever improving their environment and the ugly coating on the suits was not to his liking.

Alex checked the readings on his visor. "Approaching the docking point you identified Sorah. Still happy with your choice, now we are closer?"

"Yes Captain. It is far enough away from most of the life signs and will allow us to enter the vessel on our own terms." She replied.

"Ok, great. Buddy, initiate docking procedures."

Their shuttle slowed and drifted 180 degrees as Buddy expertly manoeuvred them towards the docking bay and there was a soft clunk as the craft docked, followed by a hiss as the seal formed and the pressure equalised over the airlock to the stricken craft.

"Power is still down on the Divinium ship. We will have to manually open the airlock. Buddy, want to do the honours?" Alex asked, gesturing towards the door.

Buddy decoupled from the floor and drifted slowly over to the door. Two of his manipulator arms shimmered as he re-formed them into two large, thin blades. He slipped the blades into the airlock seal and pumped some more energy into them, thickening the blades before twisting them to force the door open.

There was another hiss as the air from the ship rushed into their shuttle. A sweet and spicy smell tainted the air and a thin haze of smoke drifted lazily in swirls, disturbed by the change in pressure. Sorah immediately leapt through the gap and checked the room outside for hostiles. Despite the scan for life signs being clear in this area, she would not take any chances. After indicating that the room was clear, she signalled the rest of the squad inside.

19. Enemy Territory

As they broached the first corridor, the smell intensified and, combined with the flickering lights along the route, made for an imposing first impression of the Ship. Recessed into the walls were cavities containing burning flames, rather than the electrical lighting one would expect on a starship. The wall panels had a diamond lattice grill covering them, which stood out over the wall behind and caused the shadows to dance in the candlelight.

Every few meters, you had to walk through an ornamental archway to continue down the corridor. Each one intricately carved with life-size images of alien warriors in religious robes and armour hands held out before them, holding small cubes from which incense poured. Beneath their feet, a military feeling red carpet lined the centre of the walkway.

They had only walked about 10 metres before they encountered the first body. He lay on his side in a foetal position, his robes splayed out around him, only constrained by the pieces of armour he wore. There were no visible wounds on his body, and he held his hands together in what seemed like a prayer.

He was humanoid and his skin had a paleness to it, made even more apparent by swathes of ochre markings across his cheeks and shaved scalp. His lips had a blue tinge to them and a thin trail of red blood leaked from the corner of his mouth, staining the white robe at its collar.

Alex looked down at the dead alien. "Shanice, any way we can tell how he died?"

She moved towards the body and scanned it with her visor, the medical plug in analysing it. Reaching down, she used a long thin device she pulled from a pouch on the blood leaking from his mouth. After a few seconds, the results appeared on her screen. "Poison. According to my scans, the piece of armour around his neck contains a device that injects the poison when activated."

"Was it suicide? Or activated remotely?" J'Coub asked in horrified fascination.

Shanice sent a copy of the device blue print to their visors. "Suicide. It's manually operated, so he did this to himself. From how they speak, I am guessing they see it as a 'clean' death to avoid coming into contact with corruption. And by corruption I mean us." She shuddered as she stood up.

"Noted." Alex said, shaking his head slightly. "J'Coub, can you see any access points where we can get into their systems anywhere? These people don't make any sense to me."

J'Coub finally looked away from the body and met Alex's gaze. "Our scan of the previous vessels indicates we will need to access either their bridge or their data core to gain full access."

"It seems like they want neither their ship nor their bodies falling into enemy hands." Sorah stared down the corridor calmly. "Let's keep moving towards their bridge."

She started walking towards their destination, alert for any signs of life on their visors. As they rounded a corner, they saw more bodies littering the floor and noticed a door in one wall leading into what looked like a place of worship. Dead bodies slumped in austere pews, all facing a large platform. The room was vast and imposing with iron statues of armoured knights either side of the platform and a huge carving on the wall behind depicting two spheres joined within what looked like an infinity symbol. The sphere on the left was black and the one on the right was a vivid white.

The symbol around the spheres was distorted by them. The bright one seemed to push the lines of the infinity sign outwards whilst the black one seemed to suck them in. "This seems to be a representation of a supernova and a black hole." J'Coub observed as he ignored the bodies and walked towards the carving. "You have the supernova, radiant and explosive, pushing outwards into infinity and creation. It's destruction spreading material across the universe in a deadly birth. The black hole consumes. It's the end where everything is drawn into nothingness." He stared at it for a moment longer, then turned to the crew. "Forgive me. Years of assessing artworks for the gallery is a habit I don't seem to have broken."

Sorah turned towards the door. "Two life signs heading this way. Shanice J'Coub take cover. Buddy get high, Alex get behind the statue and provide me covering fire. I will try to talk to them, but I doubt they will listen. MOVE!"

The team leapt into action, following Sorah's orders. Shanice dived behind one pew and reached for one of the grenades she had brought. Her helmet deployed automatically and her visor immediately sprang into life, providing a tactical assessment of the situation.

J'Coub did the same, running to the first available pew for cover. Crouching down, he came face to face with the glassy staring eyes of one of the Divinium corpses littering the space, its head fallen from the bench behind and hanging loosely over the edge. A shiver ran down his spine, and he couldn't shake the feeling that the dead alien was staring at him accusingly. He watched in horror as a foamy droplet of blood dripped from its mouth to splash into a small puddle on the floor. His eyes unfocussed as he shuffled himself along the row to avoid looking into its face. He gripped the Tazer Sorah had given him tightly and concentrated on steadying his breathing.

Alex took position behind the statue. He had a clear line of sight to the entire room from his vantage point, but was still protected by the huge iron effigy. His old training still held, and he watched as Sorah positioned herself to the side of the main doors and Buddy flew up towards the ceiling in the room's corner on the opposite side of the door to Sorah. He watched on his visor as it showed the life forms drawing closer, a third red dot having joined the two previous ones.

Unlike in previous battles on earth, he didn't have to signal to Sorah that they were closing in. She had the same information as him on her own visor. He watched as she activated her armour. The helmet engaged the same way his did, but spread upwards to cover the sharp horns on her head, the glistening metal making them look even more wicked in the flickering light. As the Flexium did its work, the metal continued to bubble out of the suit itself, hardening into a sturdy carapace around the warrior.

Alex thought she almost looked like one of the armoured statues around them as she stood defiantly in the doorway, ready to meet the enemy head on but always willing to give them a chance to talk first. She stood, arms by her side in a non-threatening posture, but he knew she could have the rifle off her back in seconds, ready to engage.

The tension in the room grew as the red dots grew closer on the screens. Then they heard the footsteps pounding down the corridor, growing louder as the Divinium approached. Suddenly, two figures burst into the room, swiftly followed by another. They were wide eyed and out of breath, their armour dull in the candlelight. One held a wicked scythe in his hand and another what looked to Alex like a medieval mace. The one at the rear held a censer with drifting incense billowing from it as he muttered prayers. Sweat trickled down his brow and tears glistened in his eyes as they darted around the space.

Sorah held up her hands. "Lay down your weapons. We do not wish for further conflict!"

The one holding the scythe spat at the ground. His face purple with rage. "Foul corruption. You DARE set foot in our sanctum? Your sins have doomed us already."

The one next to him shook with anger, madness or fear Alex couldn't tell. "Do not address the female brother. You stain your soul further. Kill her and use her blood to cleanse this place."

Sorah arched a brow beneath her visor. "Your people have attacked us twice now, unprovoked. I do not wish to engage in further hostilities, but we will defend ourselves if need be. You have already seen how capable we are."

The mace wielder hissed. "Kill her brother! Every word that falls from her lips to our ears is blasphemy!"

The third one fell to his knees at the back, mumbling and weeping as he did. "We are already denied salvation, La'Kar. As our brethren embraced the void, their faith put us to shame when ours failed. We won't be reborn, but at least we can put an end to this filth before it spreads further."

The Scythe wielder stepped back, never taking his eyes off Sorah, and rested a hand firmly on the kneeling alien's shoulder.

"Nay Hathum, my faith never wavered. I did as was ordained, but the cleansing had other plans for me. My bittersweet never took." He squeezed his compatriots shoulder and a quiet click broke the silence. Within moments, the kneeling figure let out a soft choke, his eyes bulging out even further. "But let my unwavering faith guide you." He released his grip, and the man slumped to the floor, twitching before he grew still.

The one with the mace, La'Kar, grimaced and pointed his weapon towards Sorah. "The cleansing spared us so we could wipe you from existence. That abomination and all who it touched." The mace glowed with a red heat and he leapt towards Sorah.

Suddenly a crack rang through the room and La'Kar dropped to the ground, a red hole appearing in the centre of his forehead. Alex had taken the shot as soon as he was forced to do so and watched as Sorah dropped into a battle ready stance, the echoing of the shot reverberating around the space.

The final alien roared incoherently as he watched his brother drop to the ground, dead, and gripped his scythe tightly as he turned to face Sorah. A guttural cry ripped from his mouth as he swung the huge weapon towards her. She stepped gracefully to the side, avoiding the swing. "This is your last chance to disengage." Sorah tipped her head towards the raging man, but he was beyond reason, the scythe swinging in wide, deadly arcs as he advanced towards her. Sorah's training took over, her body moving with practiced ease, each dodge calculated and precise.

The man, driven by blind fury, failed to see the disadvantage his rage put him at. Sorah, on the other hand, was calm, her movements fluid as water. She waited for the right moment and struck when the scythe's blade was overextended after a particularly vicious swing. With a swift step forward, she closed the distance between them, her arm shooting out to grab the scythe's shaft in her armoured grip.

The alien tried to pull back, but Sorah's grip was ironclad. With a sharp twist, she wrenched the weapon from his grasp, sending it clattering to the ground far out of reach. Losing his weapon seemed to only fuel his rage further, and he lunged at Sorah with bare hands, his fingers curled into claws.

Sorah sidestepped, her own hand striking out like a viper, catching the alien under the jaw with an open palm strike that sent him reeling backward. The force of the blow was enough to daze him, but he shook his head, clearing the cobwebs, and charged again, this time aiming a punch at Sorah's head.

With the grace of a dancer, Sorah ducked under the swing, moving behind her attacker. She kicked at the back of his knee, a move designed to incapacitate rather than harm fatally. The alien stumbled, his leg buckling under him, but he managed to catch himself before hitting the ground, turning with a snarl to face Sorah once more.

The scythe wielder's eyes burned with a mix of hatred and desperation. He made a final, desperate charge, his arms spread wide in an attempt to grapple Sorah to the ground. This time, Sorah didn't move away. Instead, she stepped into the charge, her hands coming up to meet his chest. With a push fuelled by both her strength and his momentum, she sent him flying backward.

The alien's back hit the wall with a sickening thud, and he slid to the ground, the fight finally leaving his body as he realised the futility of his actions. Sorah stood over him, her stance relaxing slightly, but still alert for any further aggression.

"Your path ends here," she said, her voice low. "Lay down your hatred. Let it go."

But the alien's eyes stared at her with loathing and before she could reach he grasped the red hot mace that had fallen from his brother's grasp. The smell of burning flesh filled the air, and he screamed in pain as his hand burned and bubbled where it contacted the weapon. Sorah stood still, shocked by the horrifying scene unfolding before her, but before she could act and despite the agony he was in, the man brought the mace to his throat and pushed it in, even as the blackened skin of his fist flaked away to reveal the bone underneath.

Sorah stepped back quickly and turned her head, her helmet retracting as she vomited onto the floor. The screams of the man quickly subsided to a gurgle and a sizzling sound in the background. He was no longer a threat.

Alex watched on in horror as, slowly, the remaining life signs blinked out across the enemy vessel one by one until only one was left. They had exited the sanctum as quickly as possible, not wishing to spend a second longer in that awful place. He could tell that what had happened had shaken the entire team, but he comforted himself by knowing that they had given every opportunity for peace.

"It looks like the remaining Divinium have suicided, apart from one." He breathed. "We need to get out of this awful place. Shanice, Sorah, are you up to investigating this last life sign? It hasn't moved since the initial scans. If it doesn't pose a threat, leave it be. I don't think we can handle any more death, so quietly does it. J, Buddy and I will head to the bridge, download the data and we can get the hell out of here?"

They each nodded in assent, not trusting their voices if they had to speak. Shanice took Sorah's hand, and they moved away shoulder to shoulder towards the last living alien on the ship.

20. The Prophet

"Are you ok?" Shanice asked gently as she and Sorah neared their destination. "That was…it was..."

"Horrific." Sorah finished for her. "What drives a creature to do that to themselves when we are offering peace?" Her voice was almost pleading.

Shanice leant in and gripped her friend. "There seems to be no reasoning with them Sorah. They are rabid fanatics, blinded by their own beliefs and hatred. There were people like that back on Earth as well, so twisted by indoctrination and fear that they would do almost anything."

Sorah hugged her back and held her for a few moments before stepping back. Regardless of the cause, they made their decision.

Shanice held her hand for a fraction longer and then nodded. "Slow and quiet. I'll have the knock out grenades ready, but I'll take your lead."

Sorah tapped her visor, projecting the ship's interior layout. "It's not too far ahead. They seem to be in a small room towards the centre of the craft. Follow me."

Shanice fell in behind the tactical officer, the grenade ready in her hand. Her visor showed the same map Sorah had referred to. The corridors all led to the centre of the vessel signifying some importance to the room they were heading towards, but the layout seemed odd. The room was small and not connected to any other rooms, instead surrounded by a circular corridor.

The ship's decor at the dock and in the Chapel was grand, but the rest of the ship was austere and military. They walked past private quarters, a canteen and stores, but aside from size and basic furnishings, they all looked similar in design. Corridors still had diamond grills and alcove candles, but lost statues, arches, and carpeted floors.

"This place is so bizarre." Shanice ran her hand over the grill on the wall. "It really is a church crossed with a battleship. What is up with the weird medieval weaponry as well? It's so impractical. At least when I went to church with my family back home there was singing and great food and hats. Oh my God, the hats!" She paused a moment. "Sorry. I know I am babbling."

Sorah checked the junction to see if the corridor ahead was clear. "It's ok, but maybe babble quieter? We are nearly there." She motioned for Shanice to hold position as they reached the end of the corridor where a smooth, curved metal wall stood beyond. The corridor snaked around the circular room in both directions, and Sorah positioned herself against one wall to look out either way.

"It's clear," she whispered and consulted the HUD on her visor. "They are still in the room ahead." She motioned for Shanice to join her and pulled a pistol from a hip holster. "We go right and walk around until we find the door. Stay behind me and keep the gas grenade ready, but do not launch until I say so, understood?"

"Understood."

Sorah slowly walked forward and headed right. The wall continued curving around to their left, but even when they neared the next branching hallway a quarter of the way round, there was still no door. Despite not seeing anything on her visor, Sorah checked the corridor and signalled for the pair to continue.

When they reached the next junction halfway round, there was still no doorway.

"It's always the last place you look!" Shanice whispered quietly as they continued.

The next junction passed, and they had almost completed a full circuit of the mysterious room when Sorah noticed a strange indentation on the wall. It was around head height and rectangular, about the size of a thin shelf. A quick hand signal and they both stopped just before they reached it. The two of them could see the junction they had started at just ahead of them.

Sorah examined the indentation and noticed a marginally thicker seam along the top. "It's a small hatch." She observed. "Way too small for someone to get through, but the visor isn't picking up any other entrance or exit from the room. How are we still reading a life sign from inside?"

As she reached up to touch the hatch, a weak, male voice from beyond startled her. "Hello Sorah. Hello Shanice."

They both leapt back from the hatch as if bitten.

"What the fuck?" Shanice's voice croaked.

Sorah raised her pistol and pointed it toward the Hatch. "Who are you, and how do you know our names?"

The voice spoke again, and even though it was weak and raspy, Sorah noticed it sounded remarkably young. "Buddy told me. Just now."

Sorah stared at the hatch. "Buddy is on The Bridge with the rest of my team. Who are you?"

A wet cough rang out from behind the wall. "I'm Rafen."

"Well Rafen, why don't you come out here nice and slow and I promise not to kill you."

There was a sound like a gasp followed by uncontrolled giggling, which quickly devolved into another coughing fit. Once it cleared, he spoke again. "I'm sorry! I didn't mean to laugh, but it was funny to me. I'm afraid I can't come out. They walled me in here. There's no door."

Shanice stepped forward slightly. "Are you a prisoner of the Divinium?"

Rafen let out a soft chuckle. "They wouldn't say so. But yes, I have endured being trapped in this room for 8 years now, ever since I was 15."

"Are you a criminal?" Sorah still had her weapon pointed at the hatch. "Are you one of the Divinium or some other race?"

"Buddy said you wouldn't trust me yet. Yes, I am born of the Divinium Imperium, but I am not a criminal. I'm a Prophet." He said wearily. It sounded like the strain of the conversation was wearing him down. "I'm not like the rest of them though. I hate them."

As he said it, something pinged through their comms and a floating, green, and almost comically large 'thumbs up' icon appeared in their HUD display. Sorah sent back a quick verification code which pinged back immediately with a rather rude sounding vibrating buzz over audio.

"Well, ok. This isn't weird at all!" Shanice said. "Ok Rafen. Buddy vouches for you. Somehow. How do we get you out?"

"Cut me out. The hatch is only big enough for food to come in and waste to come out." He replied.

"We don't have any cutting tools. Want me to pop back to Star?" Shanice looked at Sorah.

Sorah smiled and pulled her rifle from behind her back. "Oh, I think we will be fine. My baby here is very versatile." She patted the weapon affectionately before calibrating it on the small screen on the side. "Stand back, you too Wall Boy!"

She held the muzzle of the rifle close to the wall and activated the weapon. A thin, bright beam of energy erupted from it, and the wall began to sizzle and spark. Slowly, she worked the beam in a large circle, wide enough for them to crouch through. Finally, the circle was complete, and Sorah deactivated the weapon. The white fiery glow of the cut fading to a dark red.

"Ok Rafen. I am going to kick this through and enter. Stand by the far wall and no sudden movements. Understood?" She said.

There was a soft chuckle again. "Understood. It won't be a problem."

Sorah looked towards Shanice and nodded and then, with a swift kick from her powerful hooves, she kicked the loosened section free from the wall. Within seconds, she ducked into the room and Shanice quickly followed. The room was sparse, with a simple bed, a table and chair and what appeared to be a chamber pot against one wall.

One of the Divinium sat on the bed with the same pale skin and ochre markings as the others, but this one was young with long straggly hair and appeared emaciated, for want of a better word.

He looked up at the two and smiled weakly. "It's good to see you." Tears welled in the corner of his eyes. "I'm sorry that I…" He coughed weakly and Shanice noticed the sweat on his brow. Rafen's eyes unfocussed and then rolled back in his head as he crumpled to the floor.

21. Endgame

Alex and J'Coub reached The Bridge a few minutes after Buddy. Their engineer had raced ahead of them despite calling for him to slow down, but it had taken them all a while to reach the front of the ship. As they entered the room, they were momentarily taken aback by the grandeur that greeted them. The ceiling arched above them into a massive vaulted space. Almost every surface covered in gold filigree or crimson detailing, and above the viewscreen at the front of the bridge, they detailed the symbol from the church in jewels and precious metals.

The crew had kneeling pads, rather than chairs, to work at low tactical stations scattered around the space, all pointing towards the viewscreen. What appeared to be the Captain's station was at the front of the room with the viewscreen as a backdrop. J'Coub cringed at the thought of the sermons that he imagined could have been delivered from there.

Buddy was at the pulpit, his systems plugged in to the computers there as he furiously downloaded the data that they needed. His body swivelled slightly towards them and he flashed them a reassuring wink and a cheerful tone.

"Well, you could have at least waited for us," J'Coub said. "Either that or build me a jetpack so I can keep up with you."

Buddy disengaged from the system and hovered over to them, sending data to their visors.

"You have to be kidding me." Alex noted. "Finished already? The entire data bank?"

Buddy dipped his body forwards and tapped his chassis as if to point out how advanced he was, adding a little wolf whistle to emphasise his point.

J'Coub snorted. "Ever feel like we might as well have stayed on the ship between him and Sorah?"

"Agreed." Alex tapped his visor. "Sorah, Shanice. We finished here early. Need any help?"

The comm crackled slightly before Shanice answered, her breathing heavy. "Oh, you know, just dragging an unconscious friend of Buddy's back to Star. Tell that tin can to give us a heads up next time!"

Alex ignored the raspberry buddy blew. "Sorry Shanice, want to fill me in? I don't quite understand."

Sorah's voice came through loud and clear. "There appears to be a young Divinium male held captive on the ship. Literally walled into the craft. Him and Buddy have been chatting somehow. He seems harmless and is in poor health. Shanice and I are taking him back to Star's med lab. Meet us there."

"Copy that, Sorah." Alex disconnected the channel. "So Buddy. Something you need to tell us?"

The robot stared at him blankly. Trying to pull off enigmatic but somehow just looking a little embarrassed. An impressive feat for something without a proper face.

"Fine! But we are going to have a chat about teamwork once this is all over, mate!" He rolled his eyes at J'Coub. "Seems like we have everything we need. Let's head back to Star and see what the others have collected."

"More walking? I definitely want that jetpack. Think I can attach a saddle to Buddy?" J'Coub suggested.

Buddy blew another raspberry and floated casually past them, heading back towards the ship.

Alex walked into the med bay and his shoulders relaxed, happy to be back on home turf after the horrors of the Divinium ship.

"Hey guys. Fancy telling me what's going on?" He said as J'Coub and Buddy joined them.

Buddy hovered over to the young man on the bed and reached out with a manipulator arm to gently brush his hair from his face, where it had stuck with sweat. Shanice was gathering data from her pad and moving a trolly of medical supplies over to her patient.

"Buddy has filled me in on what has transpired." Star's voice said. "Once you entered the ship, Buddy locked onto a quantum communication channel and began conversing with this being."

Sorah looked unsure. "He knew our names and Buddy confirmed the communication, but I saw nothing in his prison cell that would allow them to talk. It was almost completely bare."

Shanice stared at her medical pad. "I might be able to answer that one, and yesterday I wouldn't have had a clue." She turned her pad round for the rest to see. "He has Flexium inside his head. It's wrapped around his brainstem and then fans out into different parts of his brain. It's fascinating."

"Any idea what it does? Did we find any traces on any of the other bodies?" Alex asked.

"No traces of Flexium anywhere else on the other ship. My best guess is the nanites are enhancing his synaptic connections somehow. At the very least, we know they allow quantum communication with Buddy."

J'Coub peered at the young man in the bed. "He looks awful. Do you know what is wrong with him?"

Shanice nodded. "Dehydration, exhaustion, severe malnutrition, several untreated ailments because of a severely compromised immune system including scurvy, muscle atrophy and anaemia. It's all treatable, but the poor lad has been locked away for near enough a decade and he hasn't been treated well."

"Don't feel too sorry for him yet. We know nothing about him." Alex pointed out. "Let's get him treated and somewhere secure but comfortable until we can find out more."

J'Coub turned to Alex. "Buddy vouches for him. It means a lot in my book."

"Me too, mate. But I'm not risking any of you after we have seen how insane the Divinium can be. Shan, can you get him sorted asap then get Sorah to bring him to the mess hall so we can have a chat? I'm gonna go see what we can find out from the data we took." He looked around the room and met everyone's eyes before nodding and heading to the bridge.

"The amount of information Buddy downloaded is going to take quite some time for Omni to sort through. What would you like us to prioritise first?" Star asked.

"Anything related to how they tracked us and any communications since before their first attack on you specifically related to us? We need to see if we are in any immediate danger."

"Acknowledged."

J'Coub strode onto the bridge. "I have prepared one of the old crew quarters for our guest and made sure there is a secure lock on the door and no access to any data consoles for now."

"Good work, J." Alex sighed and stretched back in his chair. "We have been running and fighting ever since we woke up. We need to get ahead of the game soon, because we certainly can't keep it up."

The blue-haired alien perched on the arm of Alex's chair. "As ship's counsellor, I have to ask. Are you ok?"

Rubbing the bridge of his nose, Alex took a deep breath. "Yeah. Trust me, I have been in some insane and stressful situations before. But none of us chose this. We were forcefully taken, tortured, and experimented on. And as soon as we escaped, we were constantly attacked and pursued, even though we didn't want to engage in a fight. Now we have someone else on board who looks like they have suffered a lifetime of abuse. My fantasies of exploring strange new worlds and meeting cool aliens seems ridiculous now."

J'Coub raised an eyebrow. "Hey. I'm a cool alien! You met me, didn't you? Sorah, Star and Buddy are almost as cool. Almost."

"You are pretty cool, J." Alex met the man's gaze and smiled. "Thank you. I really am glad I met you."

The Information Officer smiled back and placed a hand on Alex's cheek. "You aren't too bad yourself." He stood up and took a step back. "You know, for a primitive."

"Captain." Star interrupted. "An initial scan of the data we took is complete, focussing on the areas you requested."

"What did you find Star?" Alex asked tensely

"The four Divinium vessels were travelling together and communication was contained within those four craft. I can find no evidence that the rest of the Imperium were made aware of our presence."

Alex sighed in relief. "That's good news and means we can relax a bit for now. Anything else for now?"

Star continued. "Yes Captain. According to their logs, the four ships originated from a point in space that I do not have records of. It seems like they arrived here relatively recently through an unknown form of interstellar travel. Initial examinations seem to allude to their arrival as the first part of a 'Crusade'. I postulate we may need to prepare for an eventual second wave. Even though they may not have any information about us directly, I do not believe there would be a different reaction from them should another fleet come across us."

"I vote we be somewhere completely different when that happens. Maybe a nice tropical planet that does fabulous cocktails." J'Coub raised his hand in the air.

"Seconded!" Shanice said, walking onto the Bridge. "Our Guest is en route to the location J sent us, Sorah is carrying him like a baby. It's going to be a long process to get him back up to full health, that kind of damage is done over a long time, both physically and mentally so it will be best to treat him slowly as well to give his body time to adjust."

"Good work Shan." Alex said. "Looks like we are in the clear for now regarding immediate pursuit. This was only four ships, and they didn't give away our location to the rest of the Imperium."

"But more will be on their way to this part of town, so we had best get as far away as possible. I heard." Shanice sat down at her station and massaged her foot. "Any idea on when they might get here, Star?"

The ship's warm voice echoed from the wall. "The second wave of the Crusade is not due for approximately another 279 ship days. However, I do not know if the lack of communication from the first wave will escalate that timeline."

Alex ran his thumb and forefinger over the light stubble on his chin. "Ok, knowledge is power. We can start assessing the rest of the data we gathered and learn as much as we can about them, but for now, let's take some time for ourselves. Shower, eat, and do what you need to do to process today. It's easy to forget we aren't trained for this, despite the knowledge in our heads. Let's just be people for a while."

"Is he awake yet?" Alex asked.

Shanice swallowed her food and shook her head. "No, I am keeping him sedated for now. He's got nutrient patches on so we can get some vitamins, nutrients and meds into him slowly to allow his body time to adust. Same with hydration gel and electrolytes. I want to keep him asleep for at least a day or two."

"Can you put me to sleep for a day or two? I feel like I could do with a good rest." J'Coub joked.

"Don't tempt me!"

"Oh, if it's tempting you are after, I could think of a thousand different ways."

Shanice levelled her fork at him. "I have a paralytic agent that would be perfect for keeping that mouth of yours from working."

"But my mouth is one of the best things about me?" J'Coub replied, feigning wide-eyed innocence.

Shanice rolled her eyes at him. "Listen, you like multiple partners, I like zero partners ok? Well, one boyfriend, but it was basically platonic.Never been interested and never will be."

Alex laughed at the horrified confusion on J'Coub's face. "When pansexual meets asexual. It's like anti-matter, but without the explosions."

J'Coub's eyes narrowed. "Actually, with several of my previous partners, the bond was non-sexual."

"Can we not talk about this over the dinner table, please?" Sorah's voice was firm. "The last thing I want to think about whilst eating is your hairless bodies." She mock gagged and then a quick smile betrayed her fake seriousness.

The team bantered back and forth, relaxing into what was becoming a comfortable routine. They were slowly becoming more than a crew and had started evolving past their initial trauma. They devoured the food quickly and used a celebratory glass of their improvised wine to wash it down.

It was just as the evening was winding down that Star's urgent voice interrupted them.

"I need you! Please, I have discovered something in the archives."

Alex immediately stood and turned to the wall where Star spoke from. "What is it Star?"

Her usually calm voice was erratic and broken. "I am displaying something from their data on screen now."

Alex turned back to the table as the others cleared their plates and glasses from the holographic display. An image flickered to life. Hovering in the air was an image of Star shown from the perspective of one of the Divinium ships.

"Is this one of their scans of you Star?" Shanice enquired

"That is just it, Shanice. The being displayed is not me. This encounter was approximately one week before they attacked me, but the vessel got away. According to their systems, they were hunting it based on its emissions and came across me instead."

"Oh Star." Alex's eyes widened in realisation. "That means…"

"Yes Alex. The Vrexen have enslaved another of my people, and I cannot rest until I free them."

Sorah turned to look around the table. "Then let's get Buddy working on that Flexium armour. It looks like we have a rescue mission on our hands."

22. Epilogue

Rafen dreamed.

He was back on his pilgrimage. A thin, bookish 15-year-old wishing he were anywhere else but here. Even though all males of his species had to go through this ritual, not all made it through.

It had been a long hard trek through the desert and much to everyone's surprise; the runt, as they called him, was still here. Although he sat away from the fires and the prayer circles at night and snuck away from morning combat as often as he could, he could hardly stay unnoticed by the others.

The teasing washed over him; it was nothing new.

This morning they had reached the temple. The rusted spears of the two towers arched high into the sky and beneath that, the two pools sat waiting ominously. The one on the left was clear and bright, only disturbed by the bubbles making their way to the surface. It's dark twin lay to the right, swirling slowly as the murky waters were drawn down through some unknown hole below.

Each boy took his turn climbing into the sacred waters. Choosing the path of a priest or warrior, baptised in the light for war and in the dark for worship. There were no other choices.

Rafen limped slowly forward, the dream as strong a memory as the day itself. He had thought of this moment since he could remember. No warrior, the light held no sway for him, but his faith was weak so the thought of entering the darkness gripped him with an unknown fear.

He didn't believe, so why was he so afraid? It was just superstition after all? A wicked lie his people told themselves, a cruel untruth to keep them all in sway. But his breath hitched anyway.

The boy in front of him also chose the dark and waded into the swirling waters. Dunking his head below the surface, he emerged quickly with a grin, to the cheers of his friends on the other side. It was Rafen's turn.

Before he could change his mind and do the stupidest thing and run, he steeled himself and walked into the black pool. The water was warm from the heat of the desert sun, but surprisingly refreshing as he made his way to the centre of the pool. He ran his hands through the waters, marvelling at how it seemed to sparkle slightly in the midday light.

He could feel the waters swirling gently around his feet but even though he was barefoot, he couldn't find the drainage hole he was expecting. Jeers sounded from the boys behind him and he realised he was taking too long. He took a breath and ducked his head beneath the surface.

It was pitch dark below, but he had done his job and it was time to stand up, but Rafen suddenly felt the flow of the water grow in power. Disoriented, he tried to stand but the sudden force of the current swept him from his feet and he felt himself begin to spin uncontrollably in the vortex.

Rafen reached out his arms and legs to try and find purchase on the floor or edges of the shallow pool, but he couldn't find purchase anywhere, it was as if the waters stretched on endlessly. Despite the rising panic, he held his breath, knowing that if he inhaled the dark water, he could drown quicker than help could arrive.

Suddenly a sharp pain stabbed at his ear as he felt something wriggle its way inside his head, he reached up desperately to grab at whatever it was, but there was nothing there. Spots danced in his vision as the air in his lungs ran out and his skull was on fire.

And then nothing.

The waters were gone. His body was gone. The pain was gone.

Rafen floated formlessly in the void of space. A planet, blue and green, hung in front of him. A bright jewel against the darkness of night.

Watch

A voice said inside his mind.

Rafen would have spun around to look who had spoken, but he had no physical form here and no control. He stared at the beautiful planet before him as clouds drifted over continents dotted about a glistening blue sea.

Witness

He felt an overwhelming sense of foreboding before he felt the heat upon his back. An impossible beam of energy shot towards the planet, bathing it in a terrible white light. Rafen watched in horror, somehow seeing the event as a whole, whilst also seeing details on the surface that would be impossible for him to make out from his position.

Witness the destruction the dark ones caused.

Cities crumbled, and forests burned. The beautiful oceans boiled away. Volcanoes suddenly erupted as the very mantle of the planet super-heated and all trace of life was wiped away in an instant.

The voice came again.

This was one of many worlds to fall to them.

Rafen tried desperately to respond, but found he had no voice here.

With great cost, we Celestials turned them back.

With great power, we Celestials saved who we could.

With great sacrifice, we Celestials held them at bay.

With great sorrow, we Celestials now fail.

His non-existent heart raced as the words echoed through every atom of his being. Was this death? His? or the universes?

The old ones awake. You can not fight them. You can not survive. We weep for you. We mourn you.

Suddenly he felt his lungs fill with air. As he was lifted from the pool in his past, he woke up too in the present. Pulling the warm blanket around him, Rafen wept.

Afterword

Thank you so much for reading my debut novel. I finally pulled my finger out and wrote something, instead of thinking about it, or talking about it. I am quite proud of how it turned out. I hope you liked it.

It's such a weird thing writing a book. Some bits are hard and others practically write themselves (Hello J'Coub!). Writing a book around working a full-time job and helping to look after an ailing parent is even weirder. But the truth is, I think if I hadn't left London to move home to help my Dad out I wouldn't have finally put pen to paper.

My two one eyed rescue cats Lola and Fin were no help whatsoever, but at least they keep the parents occupied while I write.

Massive thanks to anyone who has taken a chance on a debut author and got this far, I am embarrassingly grateful for you (More so if you leave me a lovely review!)

Thanks also to my friend David who was my earliest beta reader and sent endless texts asking for more 'pages'. He is a talented writer himself so keep your eyes peeled for any of his screenplays that make it to your eyes.

https://www.novlr.org/writer/clintgreen if you want to follow me!

Star's Promise: Book 2 of Echoes of the Celestials should be out in October if you want to see what happens to the crew next…

Printed in Great Britain
by Amazon

39457651R00152